Judah Waten was born in 191  which settled in 1914 in a sm.... family moved to Melbourne ............ until he died in 1985. He worked at various occupations and was a long-standing member of the Communist Party. After the Second World War he became established as a major Australian writer, publishing seven novels as well as *Alien Son*.

IMPRINT CLASSICS

# ALIEN SON

## JUDAH WATEN

*Introduced
by David Carter*

ANGUS
& ROBERTSON

AN ANGUS & ROBERTSON BOOK

First published in Australia in 1952 by Angus & Robertson Publishers
Published by Sun Books in 1965
Reprinted 1967, 1968, 1970, 1972, 1976, 1978, 1981
Sirius paperback edition published in 1989
This Imprint Classics edition published in Australia in 1990 by
Collins/Angus & Robertson Publishers Australia

Collins/Angus & Robertson Publishers Australia
Unit 4, Eden Park, 31 Waterloo Road, North Ryde
NSW 2113, Australia

William Collins Publishers Ltd
31 View Road, Glenfield, Auckland 10, New Zealand

Angus & Robertson (UK)
16 Golden Square, London W1R 4BN, United Kingdom

National Library of Australia
Cataloguing-in-Publication data:

Waten, Judah, 1911–1985.
  Alien son.

  ISBN 0 207 16631 5.

  I. Title.

A823.3

Printed in Australia by Griffin Press
Cover painting: The Diplomats 1940 by Peter Purvis Smith.
Oil on canvas 40.5 x 50.5 cm.
Collection: Australian National Gallery, Canberra.

5   4   3   2   1
95  94  93  92  91  90

# INTRODUCTION

The stories that comprise *Alien Son* began to appear in 1946. The first to be published was 'To a Country Town', in M. Barnard Eldershaw's edition that year of the annual short story anthology *Coast to Coast*. Other stories were to appear in later editions of *Coast to Coast* (1948–52), in the literary magazine *Meanjin* (1948–50) and in the *Bulletin* (1950 & 1952). The collection itself was first published, by Angus & Robertson, in 1952. Thus the stories were written and revised over a period extending from the mid-1940s to the early 1950s.

Since being reprinted in 1965 *Alien Son* has never been out of print. It has sold over half a million copies and has become, as they say, both a popular favourite and a 'classic'. Most recently, it featured as one of 'Australia's Greatest Books' in Geoffrey Dutton's *The Australian Collection* (1985). It seems surprising, then, that *Alien Son* has received very little sustained attention from literary critics and commentators. The book is mentioned in numerous critical surveys and literary histories, but with only a few sentences of praise or description, or some biographical details about Judah Waten. The book is often noted as the first of its kind, dealing with the experiences of non English-speaking migrants to Australia. The comments are nearly always positive but also nearly always brief.

This cannot really be claimed as a case of 'scandalous neglect'. The writers of the surveys and histories have their eyes on larger horizons than Judah Waten or his short stories. Nevertheless, the comments they do make about *Alien Son* can help explain the absence of extended writing about the book and such an explanation, in turn, can point towards new ways of reading it. We can agree with (nearly) all the critics that these are marvellous, evocative and moving stories but there is a good deal more to be said about them.

To make the point briefly, *Alien Son* has been read in rather simple ways as autobiographical or, loosely-speaking, sociological. In other words it has been read as the 'simple' expression of the author's own childhood experiences, which are understood in terms either of the individual, or of the migrant group. Both these readings have their point, of course, and are clearly responding to important elements in the fiction. The retrospective first-person narrator, for example, combined with the 'plotlessness' of the stories, does invite autobiographical readings; and the stories certainly evoke a migrant community. To put it another way, the stories are 'designed' to appeal to us with the veracity of autobiography or, rather, of actual experiences recalled (for the autobiographical self becomes the centre of attention only briefly). At the same time this veracity of individual experience is designed to be understood in a more general way, for despite the idiosyncrasies of the central family we are not to take their experiences, as a *migrant* family, as merely idiosyncratic. The stories are full of other striking characters in all stages of migration; their stories set up an array of 'migrant' perspectives which frame the central story.

This opening out from individual experience is also an effect of what at first seems an odd artistic choice, and one that I'm sure strikes many readers: that of never naming 'Father' and 'Mother' (or the narrator himself for that matter). We can think of this choice as a small example of the art of these stories, one that is really quite complex in the way it manages intimacy and distance. A good deal of the distinctive quality of the *Alien Son* stories comes from the way in which they encourage the reader to assume a position of some intimacy towards the narrator's father and mother and their community, while at the same time they keep us at a distance. The distancing is carefully modulated, sometimes comic, sometimes critical, but never nostalgic. This is what gives the title of the final story, 'Mother', its accumulated poignancy and resonance when we reach it at the end of the volume.

In one sense the very success of the stories in establishing their veracity has been the problem — that is, the source of the critical silence — in that their art has been mistaken for artlessness. Reading *Alien Son* as a simple reflection of Judah Waten's experience means there is little that can be said about the stories as works of fiction. Thus the commentators, having recorded the book's publication, shift straight into noting the details of the author's life or the general situation of the migrant. Consequently, the book's strengths and emotional range, its 'flavour' as one critic puts it, tend to be attributed to the 'background' or 'direct experience' which preceded the stories, rather than to the stories themselves. Once again this leaves criticism with very little to say. Even when we know, as can readily be established, that the stories were indeed prompted by Judah Waten's own childhood experiences — or more precisely by the *recall* of those experiences, their recall for the purposes of fiction writing — we still do not necessarily know what makes the stories 'work'.

Because critics have blurred the biography and the writing, commentary on the stories has been characterised by such phrases as 'unvarnished social realism', 'unforced simplicity', 'an easy style', 'simple, flat recounting', 'a straightforward writer' — all phrases suggesting an artless, direct expression of reality. It is all too easy to misread Waten's style in *Alien Son* as natural (as if all he had to do was open his mouth...); instead we need to see the 'voice' that Waten discovers for these stories as indeed a discovery, as something *achieved,* and to understand this achievement in terms of a specific literary context. Otherwise we risk misrepresenting the kind of achievement it was; an achievement which stands out even more when considered in the light of Waten's own writing career preceding *Alien Son.*

To argue for a closer attention to the art of the stories is not to argue that we remove them from their historical — biographical or social — context. On the contrary, to read *Alien Son* in terms of a set of choices made about style, diction, focus and structure, is also to return with a fuller understanding to its historical and (auto)biographical dimensions. And we can work in the other direction as well, using a more elaborated sense of the literary and historical contexts to return us to the stories with a heightened attentiveness to their narrative strategies.

An understanding of the literary context can be explored in a number of directions. What sorts of fiction were being written and read in Australia in the late forties? What kinds of networks or groupings of writers existed and how were they likely to influence a writer? What kinds of literary or writing careers were available, both practically (getting published and getting paid) and conceptually (how was a 'career as a writer' conceived)? What kind of audience could a writer predict or imagine?

Waten himself has spoken of the period when the *Alien Son* stories were being written as the beginning of his 'second literary career'. The nature of the first literary career would probably surprise readers who know Waten only, or largely, as the author of *Alien Son*. In the late 1920s he began as a writer in a mode that might best be described as 'left *avant-garde*'. He wrote a novel called *Hunger,* influenced by the early work of John Dos Passos, and worked as editor on a magazine called *Strife.* The novel was never published, though when Waten was overseas in the early thirties some excerpts appeared in little magazines (one excerpt is incorporated in Waten's last novel *Scenes of Revolutionary Life). Strife,* produced in support of the unemployed, did not last beyond its first, October 1930, issue. In a brief essay in the magazine Waten argued for a radical proletarian art, one which would break with 'the sickly plots, tremulous love chirpings, ecstasies, sex triangles, and individual heroisms of the writers of the past'. We might ask whether any traces of these early left-wing *avant-garde* attitudes survive over a decade later in the writing of *Alien Son.*

This first literary career seems to have come to an end in England in 1932, when Waten's contacts with both literary and political circles led him towards journalism and political work and away from what he saw, at least in retrospect, as a premature attempt at a serious career as a fiction writer. On returning to Australia in early 1933, he soon re-established contacts with left-wing, journalistic and 'bohemian' circles in Melbourne, but without returning to his own attempts at literature.

The beginning of the second literary career can be dated roughly 1945. As we have noted, 'To a Country Town' appeared in the 1946 *Coast to Coast.* In addition we can find evidence of a range of writing, editing and publishing activities which, taken together, reveal to us a literary career in the process of formation. In 1945 a magazine called *Southern Stories* appeared which included an essay by Waten, 'Reflections On Literature and Painting' (plus a short story of his written under a pseudonym). This collection was the first product of Dolphin Publications, an enterprise established by Waten and the artist

Vic O'Connor to produce *Southern Stories* plus cheap editions of Australian works out of print. Together they also edited the press's second publication, *Twenty Great Australian Stories,* an anthology of Australian short fiction from Marcus Clarke through to Alan Marshall. Still in 1946, Dolphin also published the novel *Between Sky and Sea* by Herz Bergner, which Waten had translated from Yiddish into English. Excerpts from this translation appeared in a magazine called *Jewish Youth* from the Jewish cultural group, the Kadimah. Waten was a member of its editorial board in 1946.

Waten was also translating stories of contemporary Jewish life in Melbourne by another immigrant Yiddish writer, Pinchas Goldhar. One of these, 'Cafe in Carlton', appeared in *Southern Stories,* as did a story by Bergner, also translated by Waten. It was Goldhar, Waten has said, who first suggested that he should write stories based on his own childhood, on his Russian-Jewish immigrant experience, rather than the kind of stories which he had been attempting.

His earlier work included pieces like 'Young Combo's Day' which won Waten £20 in the *Sydney Morning Herald* short story competition for 1946. The story appears to be lost, but the judges' report describes its theme as: '... the problem of the frustrated aborigine at odds with life among the whites who deride and exploit him.' This seems a long way from *Alien Son,* but it is interesting to think about possible connections with the later story 'Black Girl', and with Yosl Bergner's paintings from the early 1940s of Melbourne urban Aborigines. These have been interpreted as representing links between the Aborigines and the Jews as dispossessed peoples. Perhaps, then, some of Waten's earlier attempts were not so far from the later stories after all; and perhaps the 'breakthrough' which produced *Alien Son* was as much the invention of its story-telling voice as a simple shift of subject matter.

In any case Goldhar's advice seems to have 'worked'. But what should be clear from this brief account of Judah Waten's activities is the relative complexity of the 'literary occasion', the literary context in which he was working and in which the writing of *Alien Son* began. Waten was already consciously a writer, with a diverse and public (if marginal) literary career. His writing, then, was neither an isolated nor unstructured activity but something prompted and shaped by the contemporary literary 'scene', by its ideologies and institutions. At the simplest level, there were fellow writers and critics, and a delimited publishing economy with a relatively narrow range of options for 'serious' fiction. The places where Waten published his stories — *Meanjin,* the *Bulletin, Coast to Coast* — go close to exhausting the field for local fiction publication at this time; and despite their different editors it is not misleading to see them sharing a preference for the well-made realist story which tended to anecdote and yarn rather than complex plot.

We might note two 'sets' of influences or models, both for the short story and for a literary career more generally, available to Judah Waten in the mid-1940s. On the one side, there was the influence of the Yiddish writers Goldhar and Bergner (and we might add the painter Yosl Bergner). On the other, there was a group of 'Australian' writers in Melbourne which included Nettie and Vance Palmer, Frank Dalby Davison and Alan Marshall (plus historian Brian Fitzpatrick and painters Noel Counihan and Vic O'Connor). Through the former, as well as through Waten's own family, we can trace the presence of a Jewish/Yiddish literary tradition. In *Alien Son* we find mention of Hayyim Bialik, poet and story writer in Hebrew and Yiddish, and the Yiddish short story writer Sholom Aleichem. The magazine *Jewish Youth* suggests Waten's familiarity with a wide range of modern Yiddish writing. Through the latter group of fellow writers and artists we can see the presence of an Australian literary tradition, one felt to be a strong contemporary force. As well as Waten's personal and professional contacts with the Palmer circle, the anthology *Twenty Great Australian Stories* is evidence of his consciousness of a tradition in the short story which included the contemporary figures of Vance Palmer, Gavin Casey, Alan Marshall, Frank Dalby Davison, and Katharine Susannah Prichard.

Turning back to the *Alien Son* stories we can begin to see them, not simply as the sum or product of these influences, but as a series of innovations within the field they describe. In this sense the concept of 'models' is more useful than that of influences, in that it suggests more readily the way a writer positions his or her work in relation to a contemporary field of writing. From both sets of models, then, there was a 'pressure' towards the short story. Palmer, Marshall and

Davison, Waten's closest contacts, all wrote realist stories with identifiably Australian settings; the first-person narrative voice was common, its use ranging from a limited psychological focus to the anecdotal yarn; and the stories, while clearly literary, were also popular in address.

The European Yiddish writers such as Sholom Aleichem, wrote stories which were characteristically a kind of literary equivalent of the traditional folk tale, though with an ironic edge hovering on the border between comedy and pathos. (In a late essay Waten described Aleichem as 'the funniest and saddest' of them.) Aleichem's stories retain, or re-create, a strong sense of *orality,* of oral narratives received communally. As the products of a self-conscious literary milieu they create the sense of a community by the use of an anecdotal style of narration, for example, or of a narrator from within a family. These aspects bear on our reading of *Alien Son.*

The Yiddish writers in Melbourne, Goldhar in particular, emphasised the contemporary experiences of migration and displacement. If their stories still create a sense of community, the primary communal experience is now that of marginalisation or alienation. In *Alien Son,* too, migration is a central theme. The stories are full of journeys, and one of the main ways in which the characters are differentiated is in terms of their attitudes to the new country (the Mother and Father, Hirsh and Mr Sussman, and very poignantly, at the end of 'Looking for a Husband', Mother and Mrs Hankin). At the same time Waten discovers his own means of imitating orality, in some ways harking back to the European Yiddish writers.

In this respect his language both in dialogue and description takes on *proverbial* qualities: 'He smiled back at them like a deaf and dumb uncle ...' (p. 7); '"The devil take horses and men with good legs"' p. 69); '"If you spit upwards, you're bound to get it back in the face"' (p. 177). This is not the primary kind of language in *Alien Son,* which is scarcely folksy or vernacular in style. But it is present on almost every page, worked into the stricter, less idiomatic language of literary realism. There are as well a number of stories related within stories which resemble folk tales (in miniature, the story of Hirsh's sacks, p. 12).

It is interesting that a number of critics have taken the narrator to be a child, thus missing the point that these are tales of recall. There is a distance between the story-telling voice and the child character, as well as between the narrator and the other characters, a distance which is similarly varied, shortened or lengthened, throughout the stories. These shifts of perspective, of intimacy and distance, are what 'make' the stories. The proverbial notes and the apparent simplicity (of communication or memory) together suggest bonds of language and culture which help create the sense of a community. These effects of orality and intimacy are reinforced by the impression the stories give of being shaped by the patterns of recall rather than of artful plotting, and by their focus on or *through* the child-within-the-family. But at the same time the child is distanced from the Mother and Father, from family and community; and, in a different sense, distanced from the reader and the 'adult' narrator as well. In the final, difficult, sentence of 'Neighbours', he writes: '. . . we did not speak to one another as we walked on, but neither of us knew that there could be no reconciliation with the ways of our fathers.'

The composite child-narrator is both observer and observed, innocent and implicated. He is both inside and outside any possible community, something nicely suggested in that moment in 'To a Country Town' when old Hirsh and he observe each other: 'It was as though he had caught me out' (p. 8). He shares the 'alien' status of his parents but is also alien to them. Perhaps this is why the title *Alien Son* seems so right, and why 'Mother' works so completely as the final story. As Waten himself has put it, 'It sums up the book':

> When I was a small boy I was often morbidly conscious of Mother's intent, searching eyes fixed on me . . . I was always disconcerted and would guiltily look down at the ground, anxiously turning over in my mind my day's activities. (p. 168)

It seems to me that what *Alien Son* discovers as central to the experience of migration and marginality is the experience of *self-consciousness*. The stories are full of moments of embarrassment and shame, of guilt, of characters being caught out as hypocritical or ridiculous. Again the son is central as both observer and observed — we are most conscious of him when he is being looked at or is caught

xii

out looking — and the writing is wonderfully revealing about the subtleties of the Father's self-conscious self-deceptions. Even the horses have a role, their innocence a perfect foil for the characters' shame or guilt: ' . . . as soon as he ran out of the house he began to shout ugly and hateful words at the inoffensive horse who looked at him with grateful eyes' (p. 93). (The writing about horses is one of the least expected successes of the book!)

The contrasts between Mother and Father, or Mother, Father, son, form the organising centre of *Alien Son*. But the emphasis is not on personality so much as attitude and situation although the book is full of memorable characters. Indeed many of the characters are truly 'characters' — Hirsh, Mr Segal, Mrs Hankin, Mr Frumkin, the Sisters, the midwives, Uncle Isaac. There is often a sense of performance, of (comic) dramatisation or speechifying, among the characters themselves. This quality of theatricality, something found in the European Yiddish stories as well, is linked both to the stories' intimations of orality and to the theme of self-consciousness. The stories are also structured around 'theatrical' vignettes or exchanges, either in small details, a single action that sums up a state of mind (and a state of migration) such as with Mr Hankin:

> He shrugged his shoulders and made a remark that he was often to
> repeat as one after another of his pupils left him, 'It's the Australian
> sky; it draws my pupils away from the ancient learning. Somehow it
> is a different sky from the gentle one we left behind.' (p.42)

or in extended episodes such as the party in 'To a Country Town', the theatre performance in the following story, or scenes with Father and his horses, Father and the three Sisters, Uncle Isaac and the midwives and so on.

Above all the characters are memorable for their *talk*. In a sense, the different characters are ways of telling stories (and again this is centrally true of the Mother and Father). The way the characters tell stories, and the kinds of stories they tell or prefer to listen to, distinguishes them one from the other and governs how we 'read' their characters. The 'migrant story' is full of other stories: tales of promise and regret, stories recalling the past in another place or inventing the future, stories explaining change and conflict. And it is full of misreadings, of missed signs and awkward, inappropriate or conflicting responses (a source of the book's comedy, a quality which has generally been overlooked). It is for these reasons that 'The Theatre' is for me one of the richest stories in *Alien Son,* for it links these themes around the central 'scene' of theatrical performance itself.

In stories such as 'Sisters' and 'Uncle Isaac' we see story-telling or performance with another function, creating a kind of solidarity among women. Though the scenes are often comic, the book's sensitivity here is another of the unexpected and unusual achievements that develop over the course of this 'novel without architecture' (in Waten's own term) until the final isolated portrait of the Mother.

One final dimension of *Alien Son*'s emphasis on talk and on stories within stories, is that the different modes of story-telling and performance establish a framework for our own reading of the work as a whole. Different models of story-telling and of art are contrasted: the Mother's sense of the seriousness and nobility of art (from Biblical stories to Aleichem, Tolstoy and Beethoven) against the father's love of entertainment and pleasure (the music hall!); Hirsh's 'long stories of the past' against Mr Osipov, who 'told such different stories — of strikes and battles against our great oppressor, the Czar'; or the different songs and poems at the party in 'To a Country Town', from folk song to 'La Donna e Mobile' to 'Auld Lang Syne', each of which is carefully placed in terms of the effects it produces. There is no single model which emerges without qualification, though there are clear evaluations; even the Father's 'vulgar' responses at the theatre have their point despite the embarrassment they produce.

The overall effect of these contrasts is that they bring to bear on each other aspects of folk tale or popular art, and aspects of a 'high' literary tradition. Both are appropriate references for our reading of *Alien Son;* both, in their very different ways, give to art a serious communal or social role. Together they suggest something of the work's blend of styles.

Further, although the *Alien Son* stories do ask to be read in part as 'Jewish' stories, I would argue that they are not addressed primarily to a Jewish or migrant community of readers but to a broader 'Australian' readership. They ask to be read in the light of local traditions of the short story, that is, as *Australian* stories. Their intimate sense of audience is less the product of a limited address to a Jewish/migrant community than something Waten shares with and has learnt from the community of his fellow writers such as Vance Palmer and Alan Marshall. Again, the narrator's role, mediating between inside and outside, is crucial in the way the stories address this wider Australian audience.

There is also a political dimension in the *commitment* to an Australian audience, an audience itself conceived in popular terms (so the stories suggest). Judah Waten's political career is probably almost as widely known as his literary career. He first joined the Communist Party of Australia in 1926 and, despite more than one falling out with the Party, he remained a communist and a supporter of the Soviet Union for the rest of his life. *Alien Son,* however, has generally been read as one of his 'non-political' books. One can see why, though it has its more or less explicit political moments, most clearly in the sympathetic treatment of strikers in 'Near the Wharves' or the brief mention of Benny 'always reading books and papers and hurrying to meetings' in 'Mother'.

But there is another sense in which we can think of these stories as being political, one related to the question of audience. In a work on Franz Kafka, French writers Gilles Deleuze and Felix Guattari define the concept of a 'minor literature', by which they mean a literature 'which a minority constructs within a major language'. They argue that the marginalised condition of minor literatures means that 'everything in them is political' and 'everything takes on a collective value'. In the 'cramped space' of a minority literature, each individual or family story contains the story of the whole community or culture — its marginalisation — and is thus political.

The sense of marginality is much less extreme in Waten's writing than in Kafka's; indeed only occasionally are we reminded that, for the most part, the characters we hear are speaking Yiddish (though the occasions are always telling). The sense of belonging to a minority is tempered by the sense of belonging also to a local literary tradition and to the larger traditions of literary realism. Nevertheless, the conditions of a minority literature leave their imprint on the text of *Alien Son,* in narrative voice, in diction, in its structure 'without architecture'.

From the perspective of the narrator's recall, Australia is no longer a foreign place. And yet the stories are still pervaded by an apprehension that, as Waten expressed it in a 1966 interview, 'in the 20th century . . . the Jewish migrant has been the symbol of the oppressed, and of the migratory person.' Far from nostalgic recollections or quaint family anecdote, I think this political dimension is the appropriate frame of reference for *Alien Son.*

DAVID CARTER
Brisbane 1990

# CONTENTS

# TO A COUNTRY TOWN

FATHER said we should have to leave the city. It was soon after we came to the new land that he had been told of a town where he was sure to make money if he opened a drapery shop. He had tried to find something in the city but failed, and he was anxious to make money. The possession of money, he said, would compensate us for the trials of living in a strange land. He had ambitious plans and to have listened to him one might have believed that nature had cut him out to be a millionaire.

But Mother said that he was a cripple when it came to the real job, though others with lesser flights of fancy who had come out with us on the same boat were now well on the way to making their fortunes.

"Talk, talk," she said.

No, Mother wouldn't go into the wilderness; she wouldn't leave the coast. Ever since we had come to this country she had lived with her bags packed. This was no country for us. She saw nothing but sorrow ahead. We should lose everything we possessed; our customs, our traditions; we should be swallowed up in this strange, foreign land. She had often wheeled my sister and me to shipping offices to inquire for ships leaving for home. And once she almost bought passages for us but she didn't have quite enough money.

Father roared and stamped out of the house, slamming each door as he strode down the long, dark passage. But soon he came back, his arms laden with fruit and other foodstuffs. His pale-blue eyes blinked innocently and his stiff, red moustache shook with good humour. He was very subdued and remained uncommunicative for quite a while. Then he began to talk as if to himself.

"The country would do the children a lot of good, now wouldn't it? Say only for a year or two. The children would grow strong and healthy there."

He saw a little smile flutter on Mother's lips and then disappear into the creases round her mouth. Her sallow face was serious again and her dark-brown eyes troubled. For as long as I remembered she had always looked as if she expected nothing but sorrow and hardship from life. I somehow imagined that Hagar, the mother of Ishmael, must have looked just like my mother, with her long, straight nose and her mass of jet-black hair combed back above her hollow cheeks, deep-set eyes and high forehead.

When she spoke Father knew we were going to the country. For a little while it would be good for the children, she agreed. It was always like this; she wanted nothing for herself, only a great future for us. We were to serve our oppressed people. I was to be at least another David and my sister a modern Esther. But how could those plans be furthered out there in the wilderness? Well, after all, a year would pass quickly.

One day a covered wagon drew up outside our house. Mother stared in amazement when she saw Father perched in the driver's seat. She had never expected to see him like this. What would he be doing next? How much better would it be if we were on our way from this country.

But Father was far too busy to listen to any talk. He was piling our few belongings on to the wagon until it looked like a second-hand shop on wheels. There were rust-coloured iron Russian beds with pictures embossed in gold, boxes of kitchen utensils with large silver spoons and knives engraved with the name of their Russian maker, a four-wheeled baby carriage with a large black hood, enlarged pictures of grandfathers and grandmothers, and even a green faded samovar from Tula. All lay in a disorderly pile on top of the boxes of dresses, skirts, and coats that were to bring us that fortune which my father was so certain was surely our lot in this new land.

Mother sat next to Father on the driver's seat and we sat on boxes covered with pillows stuffed with goose feathers just behind them. Immediately next to Mother rested a polished wooden box and a large black bag. Of Mother's black bag there is little to be said. Food for the journey, a purse, all sorts of knick-knacks for my little sister, a bottle of castor oil, and a thermometer were all stuffed in there.

But the red, silk-lined box was my father's treasure chest which he had clung to all his life. All the written history of the pair, the marriage certificate, passport, birth certificates, letters from Father's parents, photos, even gold links and studs and an old-fashioned pocket watch with a blue cover studded with small pink stones, a prayer shawl, and phylacteries reposed in neat order between the silk lining around which clung the smell of moth-balls. Father said there would always be something in that box to fall back on.

Father was then a young man of twenty-seven, with light-brown hair and a fine red moustache. He had been tall and slim, but he was beginning to grow fat round the stomach. But even while driving the horses he looked neat and smart. By contrast Mother always looked ragged and even her long association with Father never made her interested in her appearance.

Father bellowed and cursed at the horses as we drove along the grey, sandy road. He was in a terrible rage, but he was really shouting at his own helplessness. It was one of my first impressions of Father that whenever he was in a tight corner, in a muddle, he would shout angrily at the top of his voice. When I was very little I had looked for something to happen when Father shouted, as the walls of the city fell at the blast of the ram's horn blown at Jericho. But now I knew better; Father's rages came on swiftly and disappeared just as suddenly.

While he was roaring at the horses, his greyish, pale face a deep crimson, Father shook a long whip that flicked the air menacingly. If the expression on his face meant anything he was about to thrash the horses to within an inch of their lives. But the whip never fell on their broad haunches; he just held it aloft, his hand paralysed by uncertainty. Mother settled the matter. She snatched the whip out of his hand and threw it under the seat. What was he trying to do? Kill us?

But Father's rage had disappeared and the horses continued in their own sweet, plodding way. They were the masters and Father was the man who held the reins. I think the horses must have been laughing at him on that journey. They stopped when they wanted to and drank at the trough outside every hotel. And the white mare kept moving to the centre of the road, which was one cause of Father's rage.

The wagon trundled on through low, scraggy, dry scrub and dejected gums while the sun, now directly overhead, seemed like a fiery disk suspended from the high, pale sky. It was very hot for all of us and the light on the sandy road was hard for Father's eyes. Suddenly low blue hills appeared above the horizon and Father said we'd be there before night fell.

We kept well to the edge of the shadeless, sandy road and often the wagon threatened to turn turtle as the wheels dropped into a culvert. Mother was afraid of the road and, secretly, so was Father. The sight of a sulky drawn by a speedy horse and coming towards us would throw her into a paroxysm of fear and she would clutch Father's arm. He ineffectively tried to steer the white mare away from the centre of the road, and finally with a great effort he stopped the horses altogether while the sulky whisked by with yards between us. Then to celebrate our deliverance from such danger Mother produced fruit and sweets from the black bag.

We arrived at our new home long after the sun had sunk beneath the hills, which had become mysteriously black with odd lights that blinked forlornly as if signalling messages of distress.

In the dying light Mother stood gazing at the dingy, brown wooden cottage and while she stood she seemed to age and her narrow shoulders to grow more stooped. Her sad eyes wandered hopelessly over the broken picket fence and the neglected fruit-trees with their naked limbs outstretched.

Suddenly Mother was startled out of her deep musing by a merry clamour that sprang round us like a wind springing up from nowhere. The street which had been deserted was now alive. Men in shirt-sleeves and women in aprons stood behind fences and from open doorways flickered the yellow light of kerosene lamps. Children appeared from all the dark corners of the street, clustering round the wagon, chattering in a language of which we understood not a word. Mother seized my sister and me by our hands and bundled us into the house. And, disconsolate and weary, we sat on chairs in a room that smelt musty with dampness and disuse. By the light of a spluttering candle our parents walked silently to and fro and emptied the bulging wagon.

Early next morning I ran into the street while Mother was scrubbing one of the rooms. I was impatient to join the children whom I had seen the previous night. But as soon as they saw me they burst out laughing and pointed to my buttoned-up shoes and white silk socks. I was overcome with shame and ran back into the house where I removed my shoes and socks and threw them into one of the empty rooms. I would walk barefooted like the other boys. And when I heard Mother calling to me from the kitchen to play in the back-yard and not to go into the street, I pretended I didn't hear.

I tacked myself on to the tail end of a group of boys who were prancing down the street. It was really more a track than a street, petering out a few yards from our gate in a gentle rise that merged with the horizon so that Mother could be pardoned for thinking we lived on the very edge of the world.

I could barely stand the gravel and the hot sand on my bare feet and the short, dry grass of the paddock gave little relief. But I was proud of my own courage and of the attention the boys paid me, though I didn't know a word of what they were saying.

We came to a shed at the back of the general store that was almost directly opposite the railway station and next to a group of wooden, ramshackle buildings that housed a baker, a bootmaker and a newsagent. Farther down the street stood, in solitary splendour, a two-storied wooden hotel with a wide veranda running the width of the building.

I clambered up a high, picket fence with the rest of the boys and held on for dear life while they chattered and screeched like magpies. We were watching a short, elderly man backing a black horse into a cart.

To my surprise the man kept looking at me curiously from under heavy lids which sagged and were covered in a maze of creases. He carried a big leather bag slung over his shoulder like a Sam Browne belt and he wore a marine dealer's badge on his arm. His broad-brimmed hat with its sweat-stained band sat as flat as a pancake on his head. The boys mimicked him in a childish gibberish as he mumbled to his horse in the only language I knew.

But the old man wasn't angry with the boys. He smiled back at them like a deaf and dumb uncle and his eyes lingered a little longer over me. As he jumped up on the cart he nodded his head and stroked his little straggly brown beard and waved his long whip at me. Then with a loud cry he drove out of the yard.

Late that afternoon we were playing on the railway station. It was deserted, although a train was expected within an hour, so that we had the run of some empty trucks. A solitary cart appeared on the horizon and soon we recognized the old man perched on top of a heap of bags. We ran to meet him. He was urging his horse on and the sweaty, velvety hide of the animal quivered as the old man flicked his long whip over its mane. We chased the cart and the boys called loudly, "Bottle-oh! Bottle-oh! Any bottles today?"

But as soon as we followed him into the yard he jumped off the cart and chased us out, cracking his whip over our heads. Again he was looking closely at me, but this time there was a sly expression in his beady, half-closed eyes that made me feel distinctly uncomfortable. It was as though he had caught me out.

From the high picket fence we watched him unload his cart, stacking bottles in pyramids according to their size and shape. Then he carried a great bundle of bags piled high on his strong shoulders into a shed, where dark doors opened like the mouth of a cave. He curried and brushed his horse and carefully mixed chaff and bran into a bin, gently pushing its soft nose aside. Then he disappeared into the shed and closed the door.

When I returned home Mother complained bitterly that I had run away twice in one day; that I had thrown my shoes and socks away and would catch cold. I would get lost; all her gloomiest premonitions would come true. Father was always blunt-spoken and he said that if I disobeyed Mother again he would take to me in no uncertain way.

It was at that stage that I judged it wise to bring out my bit of news. I said that in the afternoon I had only gone to the shed to find out if the old man was really a Jew. Mother was overwhelmed.

"There you are, you find our people in the farthest corners of the world. Perhaps this place is after all not the end of everything. We might have a community here yet."

All my misdeeds were forgotten and even Father smiled.

"Bring him home," he said, cheerfully. "Let's have a look at him."

It was not until sundown the next day that I saw the old man again. I was in the street with the neighbour's boy looking into shop windows and watching the men go into the hotel, when I saw the old man pacing up and down on the opposite side of the street outside the railway

station. The train had just gone and was climbing into the
hills that rose beyond the township. Escaping smoke still
hung in grey masses against a purple sky, blotting out the
stars which had just appeared.

When he caught sight of me the old man hurried towards
me. Spacing his words slowly he asked me in a wheedling,
high-pitched, sing-song voice if I was a Jewish boy. Immediately I spoke in Yiddish his voice changed; every trace
of hesitancy disappeared. He pinched my cheeks and
rumpled my hair with his strong, callused palms.

"Why haven't I seen your father and mother? Where are
they hiding? I'll have someone to talk to at last. I'll be able
to free my heart."

Then his voice changed and in a wheedling tone, his
half-closed eyes blinking innocently, he asked, "And for
instance, what does your father do?"

He seemed relieved when I answered that he was a
draper.

From that day old Hirsh was a regular visitor to our
house. Mother's hope had been realized and we had the
beginnings of a community. Every day at six we would see
the old man hastening towards the house, his short body
erect and his quick stride soldierly. His appearance never
altered except on wet days when he wore a long shabby
overcoat over his faded blue waistcoat and the bulging
leather bag that he never parted from. He no longer lingered over his horse of an evening; he made the horse
comfortable and left without even an affectionate glance.

Even after we had sat down to our meal he remained
standing with his back to the fire, often without speaking,
his hat still on his head, his eyes almost closed.

Father, drinking his soup noisily, would grunt, "And how is business, Hirsh?"

And Hirsh invariably answered with the same words, "No good."

"Always no good! What sort of a business is this?" Father would retort sceptically breaking great hunks of bread off the loaf for all of us.

Mother, to hide her embarrassment, would invite Hirsh to take a bite with us. But he would pretend that he hadn't heard her until Father would lean towards him and say in an emphatic tone, "Sit down."

When he sat down, always at the corner of the table, Hirsh would decline the soup and meat, contenting himself with great quantities of bread and grated radish or cucumber. His manner was apologetic and he noiselessly nibbled the bread in contrast with Father's eager, noisy performance at the table.

After the meal Hirsh would push his chair into the corner, a glass of tea in his hand, and for a long while he would stare silently at the fire, until he rose with an apologetic good night and disappeared into the night. But if Father was in good talking form Hirsh would join in the conversation, respectfully waiting for Father to finish, and then telling long stories of the past that drove Father to distraction by their disjointed loquacity. He had been a coachman for a wealthy man in Russia, but he had fled to evade military service. He heartily cursed Czar Alexander III, who was now rotting in the ground. He had come a long, hard way and his dearest wish was to be buried in the Holy Land. All his family had gone to Palestine after the death of his wife, and he was going to join them there soon, he hoped, with his younger son.

Father tried hard to bring the conversation around to business.

"Never mind the past, we live in the present. Tell me something about the bottles. How, for instance, do you sell them?"

Father was anxious to try his hand at something new. He hadn't yet opened the drapery shop which was to make our fortune. He was still selling drapery to scattered houses in the near-by hills and his faith in drapery was waning. Father looked almost accusingly at Hirsh.

"You would think from what we heard in the city that everyone in the country bathed in gold. What rubbish! I have seen such poverty in the hills and even in this town that it would make your hair stand on end."

Yes, Father's fortune seemed to be swimming farther and farther away. Perhaps bottles were better than dresses? But Hirsh, in a whining voice, insisted that this bottle business was terrible. Nothing but hard work and no return to show for it.

"Believe me, this is a very hard, foreign, inhospitable land for a Jew to live in."

Mother looked up from her sewing. Hirsh was right, it was a foreign country. How could we ever learn to know the people here? At least in Russia we knew where we stood, pogroms and all. The devil you know is better than the devil you don't.

Father rose suddenly from the table. Pointing to Mother, he said that when we were in Russia it was she who pestered him to leave. He had never wanted to shift in all his life. Now it was starting all over again. He was going to bed; it was late.

Several days later, very early in the morning before sunrise, I climbed the high picket fence and, creeping softly towards Hirsh's shed, opened the door and peered into the murkiness within. Through cracks and holes in the wall the grey light cast strange shadows over the mountain of bags, neatly sorted according to their size, which in places reached to the corrugated-iron ceiling. A smell of damp earth pervaded the shed. On one of the lower layers of bags nearest to the door old Hirsh had made his bed. Later I was to discover that his bed went up and down in the most remarkable fashion. Sometimes he slept on the ground and at other times almost touching the ceiling. It depended on the stacks in the shed.

As soon as he saw my head he jumped up, blinking his eyes in amazement and yawning deeply. He had cast aside the ragged overcoats that had covered him and they now lay in a heap at the foot of his bed of bags. To my surprise he was still wearing his faded waistcoat, and he looked very old in his thick, creamy underpants that enclosed his withered backside and legs.

With a growl he quickly ran to the wall where his trousers and leggings hung from a nail, not forgetting to pick up his leather bag, which he had used as his pillow.

There was a row of big nails in the wall from which hung stiff, white, flour bags, old coats, an old horse collar, harness and a whip.

"How did you get in, you young urchin?"

I had never seen him so severe, but as soon as he had hitched his trousers up and put his leggings and boots on he softened.

"Eat something with me. You will see how a poor old Jew has his morning meal."

He walked to the tap outside the shed, washed his face and spattered some drops of water over his short, brown hair like parched, dry grass and then he went to a flour bag on the wall. He extracted a lump of bread and several onions which he peeled, passing one to me. He chewed his food slowly and after each morsel opened his mouth with satisfaction, revealing a row of strong little yellowish teeth. He slowly picked the crumbs out of his beard and rolling them into a ball thrust them back into his mouth.

"What an urchin!" He shook his finger at me. "He has to hear and know everything."

But never mind. When his youngest son was my age he was just as curious and cheeky. What a clever boy he was then! He, Hirsh, hadn't always lived like this. When his boy was my age they lived in a big house and they ate white bread, herrings, and olives for breakfast every morning. But now he had to save every penny. Suddenly he pointed to several butter boxes that stood apart from the bags and were close to an array of weirdly shaped green bottles. There he kept silk shirts and many, many other good things for his son. He would give them to him soon when they left for Palestine together.

I was depressed by the thought of Hirsh's departure and I ran all the way home. I was fairly bursting with information and as soon as I reached the kitchen where Father was sitting, a solitary figure at the table, and Mother was crouching over the fire cooking scrambled eggs for him, I began to relate my adventure with Hirsh.

Mother became very gloomy.

"What a terrible life for a Jew in his old age! So far from his homeland and his family."

Father was blunt and testy.

"Not so terrible! You can rest assured that he's got more than we have. A hoarder is a hoarder, a miser is a miser, and that is all there is to it."

Father smiled smugly as if he had settled the matter beyond all doubt.

"Let's see if he ever brings anything to our children," he added.

But Mother was afraid at the thought that Hirsh might leave. Apart from him she hardly ever saw another strange person. With him she talked in Yiddish of Russia and the life they had left. She could still not understand one word of English and she said she had no intention of ever learning the language; she would not become a part of the new land. And when she heard me chattering in the new language, or Father breaking his tongue over strange words she became alarmed as if both of us had made our peace with enemies and were about to desert our faith.

Mother hardly ever peered out of the house. But whenever she walked into the back-yard Mrs McDougall, a Scotch widow who lived next door, would begin to talk to her in a deep, booming voice. No matter how friendly our stout, high-bosomed neighbour tried to be, Mother became more suspicious and said that Mrs McDougall merely wanted to patronize her. Mother tried to avoid going out into the yard in the daytime and only my prolonged absence would tempt her to go on to the veranda to call for me.

Father tried to reason with her, but she only replied that she could see where we were going and that she would remain what she was even in this desolate spot. There was tension in the house and Mother kept on urging Father to return to the city. Often I heard them talking angrily in bed in the next room.

Then something happened that dispelled the ominous atmosphere. Jews began to appear at the house after a journey Father made into the hills, where he had met some Jewish bottle-ohs and hawkers.

First, Mr Segal arrived. He was a dark, thick-set man who had only recently shaved off his long black beard at the urgent behest of his sons. He had been in the country for some years now, but despite his sons his face represented something of a compromise, for it was covered with a dense, silky, unshaven stubble. He drove two horses in an open lorry which, on his journeys from the city, was packed with suits and dresses for lonely timber camps and the new settlements in the hills. On his return to the city the lorry was heaped with bags and bottles tied with stout rope.

Tethering his horses to the fence, he entered our house with great self-assurance. He was no longer a newcomer as we were, but quite an authority on the new country. What didn't he know? He knew every Jew and almost every non-Jew. He travelled all over the State and from time to time he visited Jews in the loneliest places. He often carried messages to them from friends and from the Rabbi in the city. The Rabbi had entrusted him with a message for old Hirsh.

Mr Segal had known Hirsh for a long time. The old man's family had gone back to Palestine. But his youngest son had been in jail even when he, Mr Segal, came to this country and would stay there for a long time yet. Hirsh lived for the day when his son would be released. Hirsh could neither read nor write, so his son had no way of getting in touch with him. The Rabbi, who visited the jail every three months, sent verbal messages to Hirsh through Mr Segal.

He knew the Rabbi quite well. A very distinguished man from London, but a little weak in the scriptures and piety. Still—good enough for this country. He visited people in jail, though, thank God, there was only one Jew there—Hirsh's son. And he was a real thief! But when he came out of jail, if he ever did, he would be worth a fortune. Old Hirsh was making it for him. He, Mr Segal, knew that he had untold sums in his leather bag, in his waistcoat pockets, and buried in the earth.

After Mr Segal had finished his recital he began to rock to and fro on his chair, well satisfied with the impression he had made.

Father snorted through his thick, wide nostrils, "I thought there was some dog hidden in that manger. I know my guests. Like son, like father."

He would hazard a guess that Hirsh robbed the farmers right and left, the old miser.

That night, after Mr Segal's departure, Mother came into our bedroom and sat down on my bed. Talking passionately, she said I must think of Hirsh only as a hero, a man of devotion and courage. He belonged to our imperishable people. Surrounded by foes who frequently desired our blood, our people had always triumphed in the end through courage and devotion.

Our house was now often full of people. Jewish bottle-ohs, hawkers, travellers in drapery, opticians, travelling tailors, all drove to our township from remote spots to spend a few hours together. Now Mother had to remind Father to attend to his business, for the kitchen so often buzzed with reminiscences and plans for the future. Thousands of pounds were made, journeys planned, children's futures mapped out—all in our kitchen.

And Hirsh was always present in the evenings, always telling the same stories of his days as a coachman or how he ran away from the Czar's army. In his presence no one mentioned the whereabouts of his son, but Hirsh constantly referred to their future journey to the Holy Land where he would find his last resting-place and his son everlasting happiness.

About this time we had another regular caller, a Russian by the name of Mr Osipov. A gaunt, tight-skinned, sallow-faced man, he would call about lunch-time and stay until he had to go to work on the railways. Mother became very fond of him. Although he was not a Jew he represented everything in the old country that was familiar and dear to her. He was in exile, too. He had fled after the 1905 revolution, after taking part in the great uprising in St Petersburg. Like Mother, he always talked of the day when he could leave for the homeland. Anxiously he waited for the revolution that he said was soon to come. Mother always said he was a man you could always really talk to; he could understand her. He was a victim of persecution, an idealist.

I loved this gaunt man. He was so different from the others I knew and he told such different stories—of strikes and battles against our great oppressor, the Czar. And at the party Father arranged, Osipov sang and danced, happy in the company of men who hated and feared Russians. And they felt that he was something of that Russia they only vaguely knew about and loved.

Father had arranged a party to celebrate, God knows what and he invited all our new acquaintances. It was on a winter's night and our dining-room, which was rarely used, was full of happy men. A driving rain was pelting against the window but the room was warm and full of the odours of chaff, horses, and bottles. Mother had covered the round dining-tables with a red plush table-cloth with golden tassels that dangled near the floor. A large pink lamp burnt in the middle of the table and every corner of the room shone with a bright, soft light. Even the Tula samovar came out for an airing. Mother polished it until it gleamed brilliantly and it stood on a small table near the window.

Mother rushed back and forth with delicacies—cakes, pancakes with white cheese, pickled cucumber, and plates of olives. Everyone was gay at our party. Even Hirsh sat in a corner and quietly murmured a song which consisted of very few words, and a bleak, tight smile hovered over his face. He listened to the animated conversation as he sang. I was rushing about falling over feet and wild with delight at so much attention. When I passed Hirsh he suddenly grabbed me and sat me on his knees. Then he furtively pulled out of his overcoat pocket some grimy boiled sweets which he placed in my hand.

Father was immersed in talk about business and he suddenly shouted across the table to Hirsh, "And how is business? Still terrible?" And as the other Jews laughed aloud, Hirsh tried to avert their impudent gaze by burying his face and beard in my hair.

The laughter continued until Mother suggested to Mr Silver that he give us a song. Everybody knew that Mr Silver had been trained as a cantor but had come to this country to seek a living. He was a pink-faced, chubby young man who sang on every possible occasion; on holy days he had sung in the synagogue in the city. He cleared his throat noisily and sang an old folk-song with an endless series of verses.

Our guests stood up and formed a circle round him and sang and danced as if, Father said, at an ancient Jewish wedding. Even Mr Osipov joined in and hummed the tune, clapping his hands and stamping around. The weary floorboards groaned as each new verse sent the guests into a new fit of dancing. After everyone fell back exhausted in his chair, Mr Silver, who secretly aspired to become an opera singer in the new country, announced that he would sing, "*La Donna e Mobile*". The excitement had subsided and he was listened to with a mixture of cynicism and boredom. Then to cap his efforts he proposed to sing something in English. And everybody listened with astonishment to "Mother Machree", and declared that Mr Silver's knowledge of English was truly remarkable.

Mr Osipov gave us a Russian song in a high-pitched tenor voice and Mother beseeched me to recite a Hebrew poem by Bialik, which I had painfully learnt from her. Old Hirsh was delighted with my performance and, knowing no more about the poem than I did, believed it was a piece from the Holy Book.

The great din and noise brought our neighbour, Mrs McDougall, into the house. Driven by curiosity and loneliness, she couldn't resist the merriment that had broken the silence of the street. How it came about that she sang her song I don't know to this day. She sang "Auld Lang Syne" in a deep, throaty voice and curiously enough everyone in the room was deeply stirred. She sang with so much longing and pathos that for a few brief moments all differences and distances seemed to be bridged.

The babble broke loose again. All cares had vanished. Everybody looked gay and well-satisfied as Mother handed cups of tea round, assisted by Mrs McDougall, who was now trying hard to talk to her. Mrs McDougall seemed to have broken through Mother's reserve and cautiously picked at all the delicacies as Mother urged her to try everything.

Then Mr Segal arrived. His silky face wore a very sombre expression and he beckoned Father into the kitchen, whispering to him in an important voice. He had very, very grave news for old Hirsh. His son was dead. The Rabbi had just informed him that morning and he had hurried out from the city in the blinding rain.

They called Hirsh to the kitchen and Mr Segal broke the news to him. At first Hirsh looked incredulous, but as Mr Segal's words sank into his brain an inhuman cry was torn from his throat which set my sister in the bedroom whimpering and cast an uneasy silence over the guests. A moment later he began to cry like a small child and tear at his straggly beard. And I, carried away by his grief and terrified at the sight of an old man crying, cried with him. Both of us filled the room with our wailing until Father angrily pushed me out of the kitchen.

Hirsh stopped crying suddenly. There was a half-insane light in his over-clouded, tiny eyes as, without another word, he shoved Father and Mr Segal aside and ran into the darkness. He shot glances of hate at both of them as he crossed the doorstep.

They followed him. Holding hurricane-lamps they stumbled across the paddock to Hirsh's shed. They pleaded with him, tried to console him, but he didn't answer them. Quickly he harnessed his horse and, bellowing half-articulate curses, he drove away towards the city.

Our guests disappeared overnight, scattered in search of their livelihood. When I came to breakfast next morning I found my parents sitting disconsolately at the table. I sat quiet and somewhat afraid as they talked sadly and wearily.

"This is the end of our community," Mother said. "Comes the first puff of wind and it blows away. How can we build on shifting sands? If we can't go back home immediately we must shift to a big city. I can't bear to think we inherit old Hirsh's place."

And somehow Father was too weary to continue the struggle with her and he agreed that soon we would leave the township. His business wasn't going too well, anyhow, and he was beginning to think anxiously of the treasures in his polished wooden box.

# THE THEATRE

"WE'LL go and see the play on Saturday," Father said quite unexpectedly as we drove in our wagon through the main street.

"Will we go to the city?" I asked.

"Where else would you see theatre?" he replied.

It was after six o'clock and there were few people about. For as far as the eye could see there was not another vehicle on the road that stretched beyond the township for miles and miles through a sea of skimpy, greyish bush.

We left the road and took the sandy track that led to the railway station and our home. The horses knew this last mile better than any other in the world. Father slackened his hold on the reins. He seemed quite content to leave all responsibility for our safe return home to them, and the horses in turn greeted his action in relaxing his tight, nervous grip by whinnying and increasing their pace.

All that day Father had been morosely absorbed in his business. But now his pale-blue eyes glittered merrily and his high, white forehead was smooth and free of furrows and creases.

"In the old country," he said proudly, "I went to the theatre as often as five nights a week. Five nights a week," he repeated wistfully as if to himself.

I barely knew what Father was talking about. I must have looked very foolish as I tried to picture to myself the mysterious world that Father so ardently longed for. He quickly perceived that his words had been wasted.

"I'll tell you what it's like," he said.

With gestures and in a declamatory voice he described a performance on the stage and soon he came to his favourite pair of actors—a husband and wife who had enthralled millions in the old country.

"He wore a diamond ring on every finger," Father said, counting each finger of his hand. "And his fur coat was made of the heaviest bear's pelt. And as for his wife! She was a beauty of beauties, a Queen of Sheba, with the throat of a nightingale. Her ear-rings were the biggest I have ever seen and they shone like lights."

"Were they as big as the electric lights in Padham's Store?" I asked during a pause.

"Foolish boy," Father said with affected sorrow, "you know less than a parrot."

I was so abashed by his humorous gaze that I refrained from asking him any more questions, but I was excited by the prospect of our forthcoming journey, and I gave myself up to day-dreaming of the theatre in the city and the actors and actresses who wore extraordinary clothes and luminous ear-rings.

As we drew near our back-yard the gracious, long summer twilight was close at hand. Behind us the sun had disappeared into the bush, leaving broad tracks of pale gold over the sky. From far off the scent of smouldering dry grass that rose from the hot, baked earth was carried towards us by the wind. Along our fence grew pink and red flowering gum-trees and behind them I saw Mother taking sheets and clothes off the line.

When we entered the yard Father stood up on the dashboard and shouted excitedly in Mother's direction, "We're going to the theatre on Saturday!"

Her thick black brows knitted in bewilderment as she put a tub full of washing on the ground and came towards us. Just then she looked young and energetic, although the sleeves of her blouse rolled up to her elbows revealed the sallow and sagging flesh of her bony arms.

She could not help asking, "And what are you celebrating now?"

Then more ironically she answered herself, "Your latest achievements!"

Father made no reply. He led the horses out of the wagon and I followed them to the stables. One of the clumsy animals was nuzzling its nose into its companion's neck while the other bared its teeth playfully at Father's back.

"Did you have such a good day that you can afford a jaunt to the city?" Mother asked when we returned to the wagon.

Father turned away and with an exaggeratedly dignified expression he wrote something in a black note-book that he pulled out of his pocket. Then he began to unload his goods. Without moving from the back of the wagon, Mother watched him carry armfuls of dresses, suits, and overcoats into the house. Walking quickly to and fro on his big, flat, turned-out feet he soon emptied the wagon and made for the stables again.

Only on the following day did Father regain his good spirits. With a will he set about preparing for the journey. The horses must be shod, the axle of the wagon greased, the harness checked; everything must be spick-and-span for this most important voyage.

In the bustle and excitement Father forgot all about his business. Perhaps he was even glad of the opportunity to stay away from his lonely round in the bush where he sold clothes to isolated farmers and their wives.

So he whistled and hummed merrily to the sound of the hammer when we waited for the blacksmith to finish shoeing a bay horse.

I watched Mr McGonty intently. He had one rear hoof resting on his bent knee and his mouth was full of nails. I held my breath with fear lest the horse should plunge with pain every time Mr McGonty drove the nails through the hot black shoes. The odour of burnt hoof that filled every corner of the forge added to my apprehension and I counted off the seconds until the blacksmith finished his work.

Wiping his hands with a blackened sweat-rag, Mr McGonty at last came towards us and smilingly asked Father what his business was. He was a heavily-built man with a large round stomach that spilled over the belt supporting his trousers. All his movements were unhurried and all his decisions preceded by much silent deliberation.

Slowly he ran his hand over the fetlocks of our horses and lifted each hoof and peered knowingly at it. Then with the quiet self-assurance of the expert he examined the wagon. Still he was in no hurry to say whether he could do the job Father so urgently required before Saturday.

Instead he winked at me and spoke to Father.

"He's a big lump of a boy. Could do with a boy like him when he grows up a bit."

Father ignored Mr McGonty's remarks. His sole anxiety was that the job be done before Saturday and he interpreted Mr McGonty's slowness in giving his answer as a very unfavourable omen indeed. At that moment the blacksmith had it in his power to deny Father the journey to the theatre.

So, as if to soften his heart, Father, in an almost pleading tone told Mr McGonty of the Jewish play in the city that he had intended taking his family to see.

A bewildered expression spread over Mr McGonty's face. What was the man talking about? To make matters worse he found it hard to understand his English. Father's speech contained such a remarkable mixture of Yiddish, Russian, and Hebrew words suitably, as he thought, adorned with English endings, that even I found some difficulty in following every word. But at least I knew beforehand that it was all about the theatre.

At last with my aid Mr McGonty understood that Father was going to some sort of foreign performance or other. He averted his eyes from us, but he couldn't conceal his sudden distrust. His black fingers fidgeted with his belt. It was as though the strange legends and superstitions that cling round every Jew had suddenly come to his mind.

"What do they do in that place you're going to?" asked Mr McGonty with more than a note of distrust in his voice.

"Sing and dance," Father replied enthusiastically.

"Sing and dance," repeated Mr McGonty. An understanding smile flickered over his stained, darkened lips. "Like Harry Lauder," he added meditatively.

"Harry Lauder?" said Father. "What's that?"

Without waiting for the blacksmith to explain, Father, obstinately determined to explain himself, said he would sing a folk-song. In fact this was his favourite one.

I winced and stared at my feet as Father sang in a hoarse, panting voice. I was livid with shame and unable to look into Mr McGonty's twinkling eyes.

"You should come to our lodge," said Mr McGonty

slowly. "You're just the sort of man we want for our smoke nights."

Father smiled with pleasure. Now he had even forgotten about the wagon and horses, so absorbed was he in telling Mr McGonty about one of his uncles who sang bass in a great choir back home.

It was the blacksmith who brought him back to the reason for his presence in the forge.

"By the way," he said, "that'll be right for Saturday."

I was glad when we finally left the blacksmith's shop. I was embarrassed and ill at ease and intolerant of Father. But he was in high good humour and convinced that he had won over a hard, unsympathetic Mr McGonty.

Father's buoyant mood lasted well into the evening. After tea he carried tins of hot water from the copper into the kitchen for our baths. Then he sat down on a chair beside the tub on the floor, lit up his pipe, and joyfully surveyed the heavy vapour-laden room. While Mother vigorously soaped my hair and face and quickly poured water from a dipper over my soapy head, he pointed the stem of his pipe at me good-naturedly and said, "You must be clean for the theatre. It's like going to a holy place."

I didn't care about going to the theatre or anywhere else when Mother rubbed soap into my eyes. I yelled, wriggled and kicked.

"Be still," Mother said testily.

For some reason or other she had a theory that soap was good for the eyes and she showed little sympathy for me in my plight. Father came to my aid.

"Are you sure that soap is good for his eyes? What if it makes them red and inflamed and stops him seeing the show?"

Mother turned angrily towards him.

"Don't meddle in matters you know nothing about. And stop talking about the theatre. Here, take him to bed," she concluded impatiently and thrust me wrapped in a blanket towards him.

Saturday morning came at last. A hurried breakfast over, we took our places in the wagon, Mother alongside Father in the driver's seat, my sister in the back seat next to me.

My parents were dressed as if for the Sabbath. Father wore a new, spotted bow tie and a straw hat, and unexpectedly Mother shone in her black silk dress with lace cuffs, so much so that she seemed out of place in our wagon.

Holding the reins lightly, Father waited for Mother to settle herself in the seat. He smiled proudly to himself when she said, "You can start. We're in your hands now, don't forget."

"Gid up," Father shouted to the horses.

"We're off!" he announced excitedly to the air.

"We're off!" I echoed his words.

The two horses fell into a jog-trot. Although it was still early, the sun blazed down and tremulous heat waves rose before us, making the whole landscape quiver and swim ahead.

We drove through the main street and the horses ambled lazily so that Mother could see something of the town. She had hardly ever ventured outside the house and the street alongside the railway station.

A low, single-fronted wooden building with a glazed blue window and a faded signboard with the words, "Theatrical and Society Photographers, Royal Studios," caught Mother's eye. We stopped while I read out the words as well as I could.

"They must have a theatre here somewhere," said Mother.

"No," said Father emphatically.

"Why not?" said Mother.

"Believe me, Mr McGonty didn't even know the word 'theatre', I had to tell him all about it. The people here don't know anything about plays."

"What are you talking about?" said Mother. "Why, I saw *King Lear* back home not so many years ago. That was by the Englishman, Shakespeare."

"That's different. That's England," Father replied with satisfaction.

"I can't see the difference," Mother said. "Shakespeare is to them what Tolstoy and Sholom Aleichem are to us."

Father made no reply but he smiled knowingly into his vest as though to say, "A lot Mother knows about this country."

Gradually the horses increased their pace and we turned to catch a last glimpse of our township resting snugly and sleepily in a sea of bush. The corrugated-iron roofs of the squat wooden buildings glittered in the sun. To me it was an important-looking town with its two-storied council hall and large school. I had just started at the school and a feeling of warm attachment for it and the whole town took hold of me. My feelings would certainly have puzzled my mother had she known of them.

We drove all day and towards evening we reached our destination in an out-of-the-way street of the city.

There was a brilliant Southern Cross in the dark sky and the earth was hot when Father tethered the horses to a tree and with great friendliness stroked their foamy, quivering hides. Then, carrying my sister in his arms, he hurried up the steep, narrow stairs to the hall above.

I lingered behind Mother and stared curiously at the small, dark entrance to the theatre and at the surrounding buildings. The padlocked wooden gates under the stone archway next to the entrance led to a bottle-yard. A hall over a bottle-yard with wooden gates—this was our theatre.

I walked up the stairs thoughtfully. Surely this was not the theatre that Father had talked about so excitedly! I had expected something more like a brightly lit fairy castle than this small, dismally lit hall. But there was no disappointment in Father's face.

He, with my sister still in his arms, and Mother stood with a circle of friends near the ticket-seller's table at the head of the stairs. They were all ardent supporters of their own theatre and some were members of the committee arranging the performance.

I knew one of them. He was a house-painter and he had visited our home. He was a short, stocky man with big, spade-like hands. Everyone knew that he loved the theatre with a great passion and no sooner was the work on a play begun than he gave up his house-painting and went to the hall to paint scenery, arrange seating, and do all the odd jobs. To his unending sorrow he was never able to take part in a play because he had an impediment in his speech. Father said he had no roof to his mouth.

The house-painter in his muffled voice gave his opinion of the drama about to be performed.

"It's a serious play, I can tell you. It will pluck at your heart strings. Our Mr Rosen acts as if he were in the Moscow Art. He's an earnest actor, not just a vaudeville singer and dancer."

I believe it dawned on Father for the first time just then that there would be no singing or dancing in the play. From then on he listened to the conversation with growing impatience as the names of great playwrights and their plays were mentioned. He fidgeted with his watch-chain as Mother expressed an opinion to the approving nods of the theatre-loving circle. I knew he wanted to say something, but as he opened his mouth Mother glanced sharply at him and I saw her press her foot on his.

He stared at the floor in amazement.

"What's that for?" he said in a hoarse whisper.

"Ssh," Mother replied softly.

Muttering angrily to himself and grasping me with his free hand he left the circle, and we walked down the length of the aisle between the chairs.

His eyes searched the people seated in the chairs. The hall had suddenly filled. A babel of voices rose, chairs scraped, people called to one another, and children ran between the rows of chairs. Father found some friends seated in the front row and he took his place next to them.

His anger had vanished and he rose and shouted and beckoned to Mother to join us. He settled himself in his chair again when he saw her coming towards us.

I gazed at the curtain wide-eyed and my heart beat quickly with expectancy. Every now and then a hand appeared at the edge of the curtain or a painted face peered at us and then disappeared. It seemed to me that mysterious things were taking place behind the faded green cloth, mysterious and magical.

The hall became dark unexpectedly. There were more chair scrapings and coughing and then a gasp of pleasure from the audience as the curtain was slowly drawn apart to reveal a tiny stage set of a room in a house in a village back home.

Father stirred in his chair as the first actor walked onto the stage. He was dressed in a traditional long black coat and he wore a woolly white beard and flowing sidelocks. Father turned excitedly to Mother and whispered something to her, but she made no reply. Her eyes were fixed on the actor.

The old man's wife came on to the stage. She was stout with the many petticoats she wore and on her head was a wig, as became a pious Jewish woman. Out of the corner of my eye I could see that Father was pre-occupied with some thought or other. He peered intently at the lady on the stage and then nudged me and whispered, "That's Miss Greenblatt. Fancy a young woman like her playing the role of an old woman."

A few minutes later Father made another discovery.

"The old man is none other than Isaac Rosen, the fruiterer. I should have known that only he could play such a part."

Mr Rosen's great passion for the theatre, like that of the house-painter, was known to everybody. He was the leading actor in the group and he was continually rehearsing lines from the many plays in which he took part. Even when he sold oranges and apples from the barrow that he pushed through the streets he would astonish the women with different voices and faces. Tonight he was more remarkable than ever. He looked like a hundred and his voice was like the old man's who lived around the corner from us.

But I was disappointed—he didn't wear a coat of bear's pelt, nor did Miss Greenblatt wear brilliant ear-rings that shone like lights. And now the play had started I was getting tired and only an intense curiosity kept my eyes open.

Father sat back in his chair in satisfaction and all the time I could hear him repeating to himself the lines declaimed by the actors. Frequently he shouted a comment on the conduct of one of the characters, the one who wore the uniform of a Czarist police inspector and who was shamelessly oppressing the old Jewish couple. When the daughter of the old couple was to be banished to Siberia for her revolutionary activities and her old mother fell at the feet of the police inspector pleading with him to have mercy on her only child, women in the audience openly wept and my father pulled out of his pocket a scented pocket-handkerchief and blew his nose loudly and covered his face to conceal his feelings.

Later when the old couple decided to join their daughter in Siberia and her young lover made a farewell speech to them, promising never to rest until our oppressors were destroyed, everybody in the audience rose to their feet and clapped, but none louder than Father, who remained standing on his feet long after the noise had subsided.

Even after the curtain fell and people were walking down the steep, narrow stairs Father still remained in the hall, talking to his friends about the stirring drama, reliving the many vivid scenes and loudly praising the actors. He waited patiently for Mr Isaac Rosen to appear and heaped on him his unrestrained eulogies.

But Mother was very self-possessed and even a little critical. For the first time that day I was in sympathy with her. I had been disappointed with the appearance of the theatre and secretly with the play also. I was sleepy and I would gladly have lain down even on a bench in the hall, just as my sister had done.

At last Mr Rosen and the rest of the players came towards us. Father, with a wide smile and his hand extended grasped the hand of one actor after another. Mr Rosen, his face still bearing traces of powder and grease-paint, stroked his heavy black moustache with pleasure as he listened to the praise.

"It was a fine role. A real Jewish father," I heard him say.

"You know," Father replied in an intimate voice, "there was something missing in the play. Perhaps it was too grim."

Mr Rosen's gaze became cool and distant.

"We can only build up a theatre on good plays," he said severely in his fine baritone voice. "Life is not an empty bubble. We're Jews. We have to look life in the face."

Father interrupted him anxiously.

"Very true. I'm not criticizing the play. It was a well-cooked dish. And believe me, you were magnificent. But there was something missing. A little pepper and salt. If you had a bit of singing now, a little bit of dancing—say a wedding scene at the end with a wandering fiddler playing a homely tune. Then it would have been as good as in Moscow. That would have made a dish for everyone to lick their fingers."

Father might have continued for a long while but Mother tugged at his coat. Her cheeks were crimson with embarrassment.

"We must go home," she said. "We have a long way to go."

Mr Rosen again shook hands with my parents and we followed the players down the stairs.

Father seemed reluctant to drive the horses away and his last glance was full of joy and yearning. But I was glad when the horses fell into a jog-trot and soon I was asleep.

# LOOKING FOR A HUSBAND

WE were moving again, but this time without Father. The day had arrived for our departure for a big city in another State. Mr Segal drove us to the wharf in his new four-wheeled buggy. He drove his high-spirited bay with careless pride and talked to Father with thoughtfully measured words. Even Mother was obliged to admit that amongst all the recent arrivals it was Mr Segal who knew most about the country and the proof was that he had done best.

As soon as we reached the quay Mr Segal became very busy. He hurried back and forth, talked to Customs officials, ships' officers, stewards, porters; gave orders to nobody in particular and supervised the transfer of most of our luggage to the ship. Our journey appeared to be Mr Segal's exclusive affair and we stood disconsolately staring at the ship, hardly knowing what to do next.

The ship was vigorously belching smoke that quickly covered the sheds in a dirty, cotton-wool blanket. It vibrated from stem to stern with impatience and infected Mother with its restlessness. She wanted to move about and seemed afraid to stand still.

"We must go aboard," she said suddenly and holding my little sister in one arm and clutching my hand firmly, she almost ran up the gangway while Father, sweating and grumbling, followed behind with two suitcases.

Father had dressed to see us off. Just before we left home he had carefully tucked into his top breast pocket a blue embroidered silk handkerchief and sidled towards the only mirror in the house—a large oval one in a gilt frame. He stole a glance at himself and a satisfied smile wrinkled his greyish, pale, handsome face. His black bowler hat and the gold chain that stretched across his vest gave him the appearance of a very successful gentleman. Around his short, light-brown hair lingered the cloying scent of hair oil and his stiff, red moustache had been trimmed and waxed.

Now, as he trudged his way up the gangway his sharply creased trousers were crumpled by the suitcases as they bumped against his legs. There was such a harassed expression on his sweaty face and in his light-blue eyes that I became troubled by the change that had come over him.

But my thoughts soon wandered from Father. There was so much to see that my head spun. Mother however held my hand firmly and refused to let me explore the new surroundings. My little sister began to whimper and Mother's eyes searched for some shady spot on the deck. It was a very hot day in January and the sun shone straight down on the ship. Douched with the venomous rays the deck seemed to sweat and wilt; it was fiery even in the shade. Only the gulls splashing and flapping their wings in the water remained cool and unperturbed.

Father was most anxious to find a quiet spot where he could talk to Mother. But wherever he turned he was surrounded by people. As if to spite the flaming, red-flecked sun, the people on deck and on the wharf were fussily active, and everywhere harsh voices sounded. In desperation Father raised his voice and talked to Mother who walked a few steps ahead, looking into various corners seeking for a secluded nook.

He kept saying disjointedly over and over again in a pleading voice, "Whatever happens I will join you soon.

You can see that my heart breaks to see you go. But I must try again. I must earn some money. Be a little patient. Will it be any better if we get back a day sooner? But that is how you want it. What can I do? Can I tear myself to pieces?"

Mother made no reply. She was absorbed with her own thoughts and she glanced resignedly at him, smiling like a deaf person. Then she suddenly came out of her reverie and caressing Father's fleshy white hand said, "Even if you make money we must leave this country. We mustn't lose ourselves here. We should only be living dead in a grave-yard."

Somewhere very near to where we stood the winches were chugging. From a lower deck come the sounds of singing and children crying. My parents were silent and unable to look into each other's eyes. A heavy humid breeze rose from behind the sheds and we moved closer to the gangway and stared at the hurrying late arrivals. Out of the corner of my eye I could see horses drowsily resting at the far end of the sheds, and the pungent scent of coal reached my nostrils as a thin layer of black dust settled over the ship.

Some bells rang and the officer who had stood at the foot of the gangway swiftly came up to the deck. After him hurried a little fussy man with a straggling iron-grey beard. There was such a beseeching expression in his short-sighted eyes that the officer stopped and shouted, "I've told you once—the ship isn't going yet! Don't you understand English?"

Father became excited and with energetic steps he advanced towards the elderly gentleman who stood peering at the broad back of the retreating officer.

"Where is your wife, Mr Hankin?" Father shouted.

"Where is my wife?" Mr Hankin replied in a nervous, questioning voice as if to himself. "My wife is taking her daughter to see the world and before she even starts she has turned half the world over."

"But where is she?" reiterated Father impatiently. "The ship will be going soon."

"I hope she will be here soon. But what do you think of the job my wife has given me? I'm to see that the ship doesn't leave without her. I've already spoken to a dozen officials and each one says, 'Don't you understand English?' and 'Can't you read?'"

Mr Segal joined them. He had gone below and inspected our cabins. With the quiet assurance of an expert he expressed pleasure at what he had seen.

"A wonderful race, the English," Mr Segal declared in a tone of finality. "A ship with them is like a palace. One day I shall take my wife for a trip on an English boat. She'll have something to talk about for the rest of her life."

But Mr Hankin kept casting nervous glances at the gangway and turning to every officer who passed. It was clear that his mind was not on Mr Segal's words. Then some bells rang out again and he turned his short-sighted eyes beseechingly to Father and spread out his palms in a gesture of complete helplessness.

"Perhaps it might be an idea to see the captain and ask him to wait," Mr Hankin ventured.

"Well, we can try," said Father, who for some unexpected reason had been thoroughly stirred by Mr Hankin's plight.

Mr Segal intervened indignantly. It would be disgraceful, he said, to waste the time of such an important man as the

captain. Mrs Hankin should come on time like other passengers. What sort of conduct was this? We were not living
in a village any more.

Just then Mother caught sight of Mrs Hankin and her
retinue near the sheds. We turned to see them making their
way through the mass of people that packed the quay. The
noise of winches had already stopped and the decks were
lined with passengers waving, shouting, and holding in
their hands long coloured streamers that twisted, flew high,
and snapped in the hot, dusty breeze blowing from the
town behind the sheds. The sun glowered more fiercely
through the red dust clouds that spread like an iron-red
pall over the quay.

Mrs Hankin waddled up the gangway ahead of her
daughter and sons, who with angry, sweating faces hauled
the trunks, cases, and bags. Wheezing and panting asthma-
tically, she stopped at the top of the gangway and took from
her large black handbag a tiny lace handkerchief and wiped
away the sweat that ran over her face and brow. She wore
a long black silk dress with a high lace collar. Wound
round the collar was a fine gold chain attached to a tiny
watch in a pocket on her bosom.

Mrs Hankin was the stoutest and biggest woman I have
ever seen and as shapeless as a sack stuffed with feathers.
On her pillar-like neck rested a high-boned face that unblinkingly and calmly surveyed the surroundings. She
removed her high, upturned hat with the ostrich feathers,
revealing a well-combed, dark-brown wig with a reddish
tint. Wisps of her own jet black hair peeped from under it.

Father had previously told us about her and I knew she
was an extremely pious lady so that her wig caused me no

surprise. But the eyes of the people on deck were drawn irresistibly in her direction. Some stared openly, others cast furtive glances, forgetting momentarily their friends on the wharf and the gaily coloured streamers that fluttered more drunkenly in the wind.

Mrs Hankin paused only for a moment and without turning her head, said in a laboured but imperious voice to her daughter, "Come, Bashka", and then moved towards us. All eyes were still turned towards her as he sons, flustered and morose, dropped their burdens in the middle of the deck with a great clatter. One of them, the youngest, a tall broad-shouldered youth with blue eyes and brown curly hair, kept a distance behind his brothers and as soon as his mother had turned her back he unconcernedly sidled away, his hands in his pockets. He had kept his eyes averted from us and his neck flushed crimson as his mother's gasping, asthmatic voice rose above the babel.

Mrs Hankin turned to her eldest son, a young man with a fine black moustache, and regardless of our presence repeated for the last time the most detailed instructions regarding the conduct of the household in her absence. Above all he was to look after his father; to see that he got his meals regularly and that he changed his linen often.

She seemed completely unaware of her sons' embarrassment and their restlessly shifting feet. Nor did she look in the direction of her fussy little husband who stood stroking his straggling iron-grey beard, a quizzical expression in his short-sighted eyes. She looked up suddenly and discovered the absence of her youngest. Her voice rose menacingly. "Sam, Sam!" resounded over the deck. He was slow in coming and Mrs Hankin adjusted her black-taped, steel-rimmed glasses, wrinkled her fat, snub nose and looked severely at her husband as if he were responsible for Sam's absence.

"Ashamed of your mother, hah?" she said scornfully to Sam, who approached with timid steps, his eyes averted to the ground.

"Take him well in hand," she said, turning to her husband, "or we might have a renegade in the family." Her voice was still loud and laboured and her green, slightly almond-shaped eyes glittered from behind her glasses.

Again Mr Segal anxiously intervened with a remonstrance, "Mrs Hankin, why do you speak so loudly? Why do you have to attract so much attention? Look at the way English people speak, just take a look."

Unblinkingly Mrs Hankin looked him up and down and, wrinkling her snub nose with disdain, she wheezed, "Are you teaching me how to behave in this country? I was here before you were led to your wedding in whatever hamlet you came from. Because you have tasted money you think you know everything and can give everybody orders. You keep your orders for your wife."

Mr Segal's face darkened and muttering something he hastily shook hands with Mother and left our circle.

Indeed the Hankins were amongst the oldest members of the community in the town we were about to leave. They had come from Europe at the turn of the century and Mr Hankin had resumed his old profession of teaching the scriptures. He began his work after ordinary school hours and the number of his pupils grew with every boat-load of immigrants.

At first everything had been the same as in the old country. The class-room was like the one he had left behind;

the blinds were always drawn and the odours of cooking, of frying chicken fat and onions drifted into the room where seven or eight little boys plaintively chanted in Hebrew, "In the beginning God created the heaven and the earth", while a more advanced group of boys intoned with gabbling restlessness, "One generation passeth away, and another generation cometh; but the earth abideth for ever."

Mr Hankin had brought into the room the familiar odour of musty, yellowing prayer books, commentaries, and guttering candles. But his pupils were not the same as he had known before. They only stayed with him a short time and they resented losing even those few precious hours of playtime. It took him a long time to realize that the new country was quite different from the one he had left. He shrugged his shoulders and made a remark that he was often to repeat as one after another of his pupils left him, "It's the Australian sky; it draws my pupils away from the ancient learning. Somehow it is a different sky from the gentle one we left behind."

Mr Hankin and his growing family would have starved but for his wife. She collected his fees, found new pupils for him, and generally managed his affairs. He was too refined and spiritual to dabble in business matters, so as well as presenting him with additions to their family, she took a stall in the markets and bought and sold second-hand clothes. Thus Mr Hankin was able to continue to teach his ever-changing classes the scriptures, while she carried on her business alone until her first-born was old enough to join her.

Now Mr and Mrs Hankin were parting for the first time in their long married life, and he stood aside while his sons embraced their mother, kissing her lightly on her cheeks.

He stood as if nailed to the deck, nervously stroking his thin iron-grey beard and shyly cast sideway glances at her. Suddenly she looked at him and said, "Go with good health", and she squeezed his outstretched hands. It seemed strange to me that they neither embraced nor kissed and their eyes remained dry.

At the same time my Father had embraced Mother as though he never intended to let her out of his arms again. He kissed her passionately on the lips, eyes, brow, and hands and then, as if overcome by a sudden rush of sad memories, began to weep bitterly. Mother gently released herself from his grip and Father blindly rained kisses on my little sister and then on me, raising me high in his arms until I was on a level with his face.

I had all this time kept looking round and wriggling in his arms to see if we were being watched, so ashamed was I of Father's display, and I felt relieved when he at last left us and followed Mr Hankin down the gangway, still sobbing in a loud tone as if gasping for air. But no sooner was he on the wharf than I felt a lump rising in my throat and a feeling of great longing for him swept through me. For a while I restrained my tears, but the sight of Father standing on the quay with tears streaming down his face and calling out our names in a broken, sad voice released all my feelings and I wept with him.

As the ship began to leave its moorings a small band struck up "Until We Meet Again", and some passengers joined in the chorus. My mind strayed from Father to the band, which consisted of a violin, cornet, and drum. A small boy in a cap that fell over his ears and a navy-and-white sailor's collar blew the accompaniment on the cornet, a pig-tailed girl drummed ceaselessly while a grown man played the melody on the violin with a short bowing move-ment. The fiddler acknowledged the money thrown to him by passengers by lightly tipping the peak of his grey cloth cap.

The sound of the band followed us down stream. Even as the ship was turned by a fussy, self-important tug and the quay suddenly disappeared from view the plaintive strains of the violin were taken up by the passengers who still lined the deck.

Soon we were out in the open sea. Over the quickly re-ceding shore rose dome-like, great masses of red dust-clouds that slowly reached out towards us. The seagulls flew high over the stern as if on escort duty. The fiery red sun was now quickly travelling to its resting place behind the horizon and a grey, feathery haze rose just ahead of us. The ship's siren had hooted its last farewell to the land and strange bells rang out frequently. Bustling stewards were still re-moving luggage from the deck and directing passengers to various parts of the ship. But Mother, nursing my little sister, Mrs Hankin and her daughter, Bashka, remained seated in their chairs in a tiny alcove of the deck as if they had nowhere to go.

As a melodious gong sounded for dinner Mrs Hankin shook her head, "I wouldn't go down to the dining-room if you paid me."

She ordered Bashka to bring her a Gladstone bag that opened like a concertina and she drew out a boiled chicken, some pickled cucumbers, a loaf of bread, a bottle of pre-served cherries, and some serviettes, and proceeded to lay a table on a low stool that was found somewhere or other. I was torn between a desire to follow the rest of the people

to the dining-room and a vagrant appetite for the good
things that Mrs Hankin had taken out.

Hastily chewing on a bit of chicken thrust into my hand
I begged Mother to let me go. Mother said she was afraid
to let me go to the dining-room on my own. I might get
hurt walking down the staircase or, God forbid, I might
fall into the sea. But Mother was not really determined
about her objections; she simply wanted me by her side.
The more persistently I argued the more she wavered.

"Very well," she said. "You can go if Bashka goes with
you."

Mrs Hankin wouldn't hear of her daughter descending
into that Christian pit of iniquity, where milk and meat
were served together and all meats cooked in pig fat. "You
can go tomorrow," said Mother and as if to appease Mrs
Hankin she added that allowances must be made for a boy
who had not yet reached his Bah-Mitzvah. He would not
be thirteen for some years and if in the meantime he was
sinning, his father would gladly carry the burden of those
sins.

So I was obliged to sit with them and although I ate
with wolfish pleasure I stared sulkily at the darkening
waves that gaily played round the ship. As more people
passed us with quizzical glances my sulkiness quickly turned
to embarrassment and I became absorbed in thoughts of
how to escape.

All this time Bashka was as silent as the tomb. She must
then have been about twenty-five years old, plump and
short with a snub nose like her mother's. It was possible to
see something of what her mother had once looked like.
But Bashka's eyes were like round, dark pools and full of a
great yearning while her mother's eyes were green and

slightly almond-shaped and glittered with impatience without ever seeming to blink. It was hard to say whether
Bashka ever resented her mother's loud, wheezy orders. She
seemed to have no life of her own; her mother decided everything. Until midnight, when we all retired to our cabins,
Bashka waited hand and foot on her mother.

Next morning I rose early and ran quickly on deck. The
sea lay calmly in a grey-green bed and from afar the smoke
of some passing ship hung suspended in the sky. The gruff
but friendly voices of sailors swabbing the deck drew me
towards them and I followed as they walked bare-footed to
their quarters. I began to picture myself as a sailor and then
and there I resolved to go to sea as soon as I grew up. This
pleasant day-dream passed in an instant for out of the
corner of my eye I saw Mrs Hankin and Bashka sitting in
their chairs with the Gladstone bag at their feet in the
same alcove of the deck.

I slipped past them nonchalantly with my head turned
towards the sea as soon as Mrs Hankin began rummaging
in her bag. She had discarded her elegant black silk dress
and was now wearing what might be called her seaside
clothes. A loose, yellow, pleated gown like a nightshirt
hung from her shoulders and round her middle stretched a
broad leather belt with a bunch of keys attached to it. On
her bewigged head sat flatly a floppy hat like an old-fashioned swimming cap. I had a curious feeling that her impatient eyes from behind her black-taped, steel-rimmed
glasses were boring into my back.

But as Mother was down in her cabin I felt free to roam
the ship. Soon I came across a group of boys playing with
quoits on the poop deck. They scarcely looked at me; I
could see that they were all hardened salts while I was only

a new-comer, a landlubber. I stood alone watching them from a respectful distance until one boy who was not taking part in the game strolled over to me and in an off-hand tone asked me my name and where I came from.

In exchange for my information he told me his name was Tom and he was an orphan. His uncle and aunt, who were immigrants from England, were taking him to Sydney with their family. Solemnly he questioned me on my knowledge of the ship and I confess my ears burned with shame as I stammered something that plainly showed me up as a duffer.

All the time he spoke he turned his eyes upwards and only now and again did he sneak a furtive look at me as if to weigh me up. After the cross-examination was over he announced that he would show me the various interesting places, including the wheel-house where we could play at captains and sailors and of course he would be the captain. Then, lowering his voice, he told me of a sailor who lived in the fo'c'sle, and was a great friend of his. This was a great secret that he kept from the other boys. Perceiving the impression he had made on me he added that if I happened to turn out all right he would one day take me down to the fo'c'sle. I was so overcome with gratitude that I was almost speechless.

We were about to start on our expedition to the wheel-house when to my horror Bashka appeared on the poop deck. She was dressed in a dark brown costume with a white satin blouse as though she was about to leave the ship, but her lace petticoat just peeped out from under her skirt. Her hair, an unruly mass of tight, shiny black curls stirred in the cool breeze that swept across the ship. Her gentle gaze roamed the deck and in the mildest of voices she said, "Your mother wants you."

I fled, neither looking this way nor that, pursued by Bashka who broke into a funny little short-strided run. She soon caught up with me and I poured out to her my indignation and shame. Why wasn't I treated as other boys were?

"Because you are different," replied Bashka quietly.

But for the life of me I couldn't see how I was different from the boys I had left on the poop deck. But Bashka knew it was so.

I began to envy Tom his freedom and his knowledge of ever so many things. It seemed to me that so remarkable a boy could have as many friends as he wished. But it didn't take me long to discover that he was as friendless as I was and as eager for my company as I was for his. We roamed the ship together, made plans for going to sea and swore eternal friendship.

I said nothing to Mother about him, afraid that she might prevent me from seeing him again. I said nothing to Tom about my mother, almost pretending that she was not on the ship. I was vague about my parents and tried to convey the idea that I hated them and wished that I too were an orphan. Whenever we strolled round the deck I purposely avoided the familiar alcove where Mother sat with Mrs Hankin and Bashka. Whether my obvious avoidance of that part aroused Tom's curiosity I can't say, but one day he obstinately demanded that we go precisely in that direction. I deferred to him in this as in all other things.

Again, as on that morning when I pretended I didn't see Mrs Hankin, I deliberately looked far away into the horizon, but this time Mother was sitting there as well. I excitedly pointed to a speck on the horizon to divert Tom's attention, but all the time I could hear my mother's subdued voice and Mrs Hankin's loud asthmatic wheeze. I thought that I had steered Tom successfully away from the danger spot when I heard Mrs Hankin's voice calling to me, "Come here, young man! Come and say good morning to us!"

To some of the passengers parading the deck just then the little group in deck-chairs must have been a curious sight, for I saw glances exchanged and there was some amused whispering. Shameful thoughts of hiding, running away, pretending to be deaf, whirled through my mind, but I was cornered and irresolutely I edged towards the alcove, followed by Tom whose interest had been aroused by the foreign speaking voice. Mother looked up questioningly at me and Mrs Hankin's high-boned face with the pouches under her eyes wrinkled into an ironical smile.

"One day you can't see me, and the next day you can't even see your own mother. Tut tut, tu tu. You have begun well, young man," Mrs Hankin said, her head slightly cocked to one side and her steady, glittering eyes moved sharply from me to Tom who with mouth half open was waiting for one comprehensible word.

Her sharp glance had taken in Tom's appearance; his clothes fashioned out of an adult's cast-off suit, his thick-soled, clumsy boots and coarse black stockings. For the first time I saw him as a lonely immigrant boy and not the remarkably fortunate lad whom I so ardently envied.

"If you don't want to see your mother now," Mrs Hankin continued more brusquely, "just what will you do in twenty years' time?"

I turned pleadingly to Mother, but she remained silent and merely lowered her eyes. Her face had clouded and a frown spread from her deep-set eyes over her long straight nose that now seemed to stand out more sharply from her lined, parched face. Meantime, Mrs Hankin nodded her head with an air of sorrow and, turning to Tom, spoke English for the first time.

"And are you ashamed of your mother, too, my quiet young man?"

The abruptness of the question caused Tom to flinch and he stood tongue-tied and unable to produce any sounds. On his sallow, grubby face and in his nimble eyes there was such a bewildered expression that Mrs Hankin and Mother sat up suddenly and looked inquiringly at him.

"He's an orphan boy," I interposed proudly. I sidled closer to him and looked him up and down with the eyes of a patron. My spirits recovered; I looked at Mrs Hankin with an air of triumph as if my association with Tom called for an immediate reward.

"An orphan! An orphan!" Mother and Mrs Hankin exclaimed together, and Mrs Hankin began to rummage in her bag. Suddenly remembering something she looked up and said, "Bashka, go down to the cabin and bring up the chocolate."

After this Tom and I spent more of our time with Mother and the Hankins. We sat on the deck at their feet and Mrs Hankin, who made quite a fuss of Tom, always had something for him to chew.

For hours Tom chattered of his long journey across the seas, of the orphanage in London, of his parents he had never known, and of his innumerable relatives who had clubbed together to send him to Australia with his uncle and aunt. Mother, without understanding much of what Tom was saying, listened patiently, while occasionally Mrs Hankin muttered to herself in Yiddish, "A pity, an orphan."

The gentle movement of the ship, the endless expanse of calm sea, the cool breeze that swept in from the icy southern regions, and her agreeable companions all combined to put Mother in a more restful frame of mind. Seemingly all her anxieties had deserted her for once. She even began to enjoy the journey. But she wished that the ship could take her back now to her homeland. But with God's help we could soon return. She expressed that wish with so much fervour that her parched cheeks glowed warmly.

Mrs Hankin felt no such longing. She was determind to return to her husband and sons as soon as she had successfully accomplished her mission. And that mission was nothing more nor less than to find a husband for Bashka.

While Mother and Mrs Hankin gravely discussed the possibilities of finding the right husband for her in one of the larger Jewish communities, Bashka sat near them and listened as though she were a stranger. Mrs Hankin had letters of introduction to many eminent people, rabbis, teachers of scripture, and others who might assist her in her enterprise. With a cunning expression in her unblinking, green eyes she said that she wasn't particular whether the prospective husband was religious or not. She knew that few of the young people were genuinely pious and she bowed to fate in this.

But he must be a Jew. That was all she asked; that was all the qualifications required. As for those people who talked about love, she scorned them. She herself had never known her husband before their marriage yet they had lived the best part of their life in great happiness. Bashka would make a good wife, of that she was certain. It had been regrettably impossible to find a husband for Bashka back home, but Mrs Hankin, who was quite sure that marriages were arranged in heaven, was equally confident that Bashka had not been overlooked.

On the night before we reached our first port Mother and Mrs Hankin sat talking in the darkening alcove. A black sky stretched overhead and the hot sea was lit up by phosphorescent waves that sluggishly brushed against the sides of the ship.

Far away the lights of some settlement blinked faintly, the first shore lights we had seen for many days. From the unseen land blew a desultory breeze laden with the scents of gum-trees and burning timber. A restlessness seized some of the passengers and they leaned over the taffrail avidly searching for the far-off shore.

Near the saloon a part of the deck had been roped off for a farewell dance and sing-song. Strings of Chinese lanterns and coloured streamers decorated the enclosure and a pianist and violinist played dance music while between dances an energetic tenor led the people in singing. Attracted by the sounds of singing that rose above the constant chugging of the engines I forced a reluctant Bashka to leave the alcove. I held her firmly by the hand and she timidly followed, all the time looking back lest her mother should call her for some errand or other.

We stood on the outskirts of the crowd and listened to the songs and watched the waltzers stagger with every convulsive list of the ship. Everything seemed to please Bashka and her soft, dark eyes glistened with excitement. During a pause between dances a young man with straight brown hair parted in the middle and a high white collar tightly enclosing a well-developed neck, made towards Bashka and in a cheerful voice invited her to take the next dance with him. Bashka started back, blushed crimson, and stammered something in an alarmed tone. The young man reiterated his request but fear suddenly spread over her face as if something dreadful had been proposed to her.

Bashka's perfectly good English completely forsook her and she exclaimed to me in Yiddish, "What does he want of me?"

Without awaiting a reply she fled from the astonished young man. I ran after her and when she regained her composure she begged me to say nothing about the incident. Should the merest whisper reach her mother's ears poor Bashka would never hear the end of it. She sat down in her deck-chair near Mother and Mrs Hankin with a sigh.

From the merry-makers came sounds of singing and Mrs Hankin, pointing in their direction, asked Bashka, "Well, what did you see?" She remained silent and only shrugged her shoulders. During the rest of the evening she didn't seem to listen to the conversation but from time to time she cast curious glances in the direction of the dancers.

Early next morning, as soon as the ship had tied up and the gangway was lowered, the Hankins were among the first to go ashore. Mrs Hankin, armed with her letters of introduction, was anxious to fire the first shots of her campaign; if her efforts were crowned with an even remote possibility of success she would leave the boat, arrange the marriage settlement quickly, then return to her husband and sons, leaving Bashka in very safe hands pending the wedding that must not be long delayed. In her own language, she wanted Bashka off the stage and besides, her housewifely feelings rebelled at the thought of her husband and sons left to themselves in the house that she had left for the first time.

All that morning Mother, with my sister and me at her side, wandered round the deserted decks. Everybody had gone ashore, even Tom, and Mother wouldn't allow me out of her sight lest I should fall down an open hatch. Wherever we went we heard the winches chugging and orders being shouted.

Mother was unusually brusque and absorbed in moody thought. From the deck we could see across the glistening galvanized-iron roofs of the sheds to the town beyond. Row upon row of silent wooden cottages crouched amidst sooty factories and desolate swampy paddocks near by teemed with gulls and pigeons. How different Mother had become since the ship was tied to the wharf!

She looked round at the inhospitable surroundings with such a lost expression that I became anxious to see Mrs Hankin and Bashka again.

They returned soon after lunch. Mrs Hankin's heavy body quivered with rage and scorn. Bashka's heaven-arranged mate was not to be found in this town. Someone Mrs Hankin had met had told her of a bachelor who was not averse to marriage. She had gone out on her own to see this gentleman who kept a shop in a suburb.

And what a shop! A dingy shop, stuffed with rubbish. He wanted a dowry much beyond Mrs Hankin's means. What didn't he want? she asked of nobody in particular. He wanted everything she possessed, but she gave him a fig, and as if he was something to look at! Or as if he came of a fine and learned family! An ignorant shopkeeper with nothing but money on the brain. And old—why, he was nearly as old as Mrs Hankin herself!

While Mrs Hankin was telling Mother about her unhappy experiences, Bashka remained much as always, neither gay nor sad and seemingly as aloof from her mother's anxieties as might be any stranger. She smiled gently at Tom, who with screwed-up eyes and a strained expression on his face was trying to make out even one word of Mrs Hankin's angry story. But he soon gave up the attempt and began telling Bashka of his great adventure in the city. I listened with one ear to Mrs Hankin and with the other to Tom telling of his visit to the zoo where he had seen kangaroos carrying their young in pouches.

Something Mrs Hankin said about Bashka's would-be husband made Mother laugh.

"You should thank God, Mrs Hankin, that Bashka has been saved from such a monster," Mother said. "You should laugh with happiness," she added, wiping away tears that had suddenly appeared in the corners of her eyes.

"Very true," replied Mrs Hankin. "God has been good to us."

Her anger vanished and she seemed relieved at her failure. Who wants to part with such a precious daughter? Yet is it not commanded in heaven that we be fruitful and multiply? Mrs Hankin despite the stirrings of her motherly heart knew where her duty lay. There were many more cities to explore and who could tell where Bashka's fate would be decided?

We continued our journey and the ship sailed so close to the shore that it seemed we could stretch out our hands and touch the tops of the trees that bent towards us. It grew hotter. The sun glared at us through flinty clouds that hung just above the masts. Mrs Hankin sat in her deck-chair, panting and gasping in the heat, speaking in a stifled voice as if she was choking and fanning herself with a brightly painted Chinese fan. Bashka ran backwards and forwards refilling decanters with cold water for her mother.

Towards evening a strong wind blew from the north and the ship began to toss and roll. Presently peals of thunder were heard from far away and the water rose noisily and swirled round the ship. Angry waves reached up towards the deck and some passengers hurried down to their cabins.

Mrs Hankin refused to stir. By contrast with Mother, who looked fresh and cool in a tight-waisted white skirt and a tussore silk blouse with long sleeves, and yet was agitated; Mrs Hankin, her face moist and red, and her dress round her armpits and under her breasts stained with sweat, was self-possessed and unchanged.

"The storm will pass," she said, nodding her head at Mother. "Why should we move?"

We should stay as long as it got no worse, Mother decided. She was reluctant to leave Mrs Hankin, and we all stayed in the alcove, which was safe from the waves that occasionally washed the deck. We sat huddled together, sliding backwards and forwards with each movement of the ship. Tom found us and, sitting with crossed legs in the middle of the deck, shouted with pleasure as he rolled towards the taffrail.

"Come back," Mrs Hankin wheezed. "My God, the orphan will be lost if someone doesn't keep an eye on him! Here, sit next to me."

But it was Mrs Hankin who slipped farther down the deck than we did and impatiently she sent Bashka down to the cabin for a piece of rope that was wrapped round a suitcase.

She tied the rope round her middle and attached it to a wooden rail behind her that ran the length of the deck. When her chair lurched forward the rope prevented her from sliding the whole length of the deck, but when the ship rolled back she crashed against the side of the alcove. An officer passed us and, perceiving Mrs Hankin's battle with the elements, urged us to go inside the saloon. She waved him away with her hand and in a breathless voice exclaimed, "Thank you, thank you! We're all right here."

Whilst Mrs Hankin was sliding backwards and forwards Mother again referred to the failure of her mission at the last port. Mother was not at all confident of the success of this unusual journey. The very fact that Mrs Hankin was obliged to make such a journey to find a husband for Bashka showed how different was the life here from that back home. If Mrs Hankin would take her advice she would take Bashka to the old world where she would find a young man who would love her and be worthy of such a treasure as she was.

But Mrs Hankin wouldn't hear Mother's arguments. As her chair moved backwards she bent slightly forward to get a better view of the sea; unlike Mother she enjoyed the turbulent waves and her confidence was quite unshaken. Why should she take Bashka to the old world? We belonged here now. She would find a husband for her daughter here. Mrs Hankin would stay here for ever and stay exactly as she was. And Bashka would walk in her ways.

And that was where she was wrong, Mother retorted. The old ways couldn't be kept here.

"They will be," said Mrs Hankin. "Let the world take it this way or that!"

Thus my mother and Mrs Hankin talked until the waters calmed down and the wind died away beyond the lights that still flickered on the shore. Tomorrow morning we would land and go on for ever our different ways—Mother to beat her wings against an enclosing wall and Mrs Hankin to go on relentlessly upholding the old ways in the new land.

# ON A BOTTLE-CART

It was on a cold and cheerless autumn evening that Father unexpectedly arrived.

"I've come sooner than I thought," he said. He stretched out his hand uncertainly and turned away. "It doesn't seem to go for me in this new land. Perhaps in this big city our luck will change," he added.

Mother wept noiselessly as she embraced Father. Wiping her nose with Father's handkerchief, which she had taken from his breast pocket, she whispered, "It's so much better that you have come sooner. Together we can do something. What good could come from you wandering alone in the wilderness?"

We went into the kitchen at the end of the long, dark corridor. Every room we passed was like an icy cave and only the kitchen was filled with warmth and light. The pink lamp with the long carved stem cast a wide circle of soft, rose-tinted light over the table. The big black kettle hissed on the stove.

Mother fussed round him as Father held my little sister in his arms and caressed her face with his soft, wet lips.

"Sit down. I'll get some herring and white cheese. Would you like some chicken soup?"

Then she called me sharply, "Go, get some bread for your father."

They talked together, constantly interrupting one another while I stealthily looked into Father's bags, hoping for strange and unusual presents. Mother, supporting her cheek on her palm, listened to Father's account of the miserable days he had spent travelling with drapery. She grieved that he looked so pale and had lost weight.

"Perhaps in a few months we can go away from here altogether?" she said quietly.

"Who knows?" Father said, and he averted his gaze. "In the meantime I must look round for something to do. Rothschild won't feed us," he added.

Early next morning Father dressed quickly and announced that he was calling on a certain gentleman who kept a bottle-yard. He had known Mr Frumkin long ago, before they came to this country, and now it appeared that he was a successful dealer in horses, carts, and bottles. Mr Frumkin would help him, even with money, to make a start here. I clung to Father and, observing that he was by no means displeased with my attentions, suggested to Mother that I be allowed to go with him.

Mother said that I should go to school; I had only recently started at the city school and interruption would put me back. It was a puzzle to me why Mother, who was constantly displeased when I spoke the new language in preference to the language she spoke, should be anxious that I shine at school.

"Let him go with me, this once. I haven't seen him for such a long time," Father said and his blue eyes twinkled mellowly.

He smiled pacifically at Mother and she yielded without saying another word. She followed us to the door. Her hands fussily buttoned my coat and straightened my cap while she warned Father to keep an eye on me crossing the road.

Despite my impatience with Mother's seeming reluctance to let me go, my heart felt light and I was certain that life was good and free from care. As we walked down the street I pointed out the house where Mother's new acquaintance, Miss Cohen, lived, and the school where scores of boys and girls played gaily on the gravel playground. I was glad to be in Father's company and as we passed the school I waved proudly to some acquaintance as if to say, "See here, I have a father and, what is more, a bigger and stronger one than yours."

The morning rawness set Father shivering. He was unused to the cold, since lately he had travelled in very hot parts. He grumbled that he missed the warmth as he glanced down a broad road leading to the city. Over the tall buildings in the distance hung a mist and above it sprawled grey blankets of cloud. Father's early good mood evaporated the nearer we came to the bottle-yard. He lingered before shop windows and muttered fretfully.

But as we entered the yard and saw a short, stout man poking round a stack of brown-tinted bottles, Father cried out good-humouredly, "Peace be with you, Mr Frumkin."

"Welcome, my good friend," replied Mr Frumkin and he approached us slowly, gazing at us with a sidelong squint. "I see you have brought your heir," he added slyly. As he spoke he cocked his head like an intelligent bird.

"A fine boy," Father grunted with pride.

"Come here." He turned to me. "Let Mr Frumkin have a good look at you. What are you so suddenly shy for?"

Then with a laugh he said, "His mother tells me he's a good scholar. He knows that two and two make four."

"That's very good. Always remember that two and two make four," Mr Frumkin wagged a thick, grubby finger at me.

"You should hear the way he says his prayers before he goes to bed. Like a cantor," Father boasted, staring fixedly into Mr Frumkin's face as if attempting to discover what impression his words had made.

Father had completely forgotten the purpose of his visit here and with a smile on his face he said excitedly, "Come, let Mr Frumkin hear you recite your prayers."

I was so embarrassed by Father's command and Mr Frumkin's sly, squinting gaze that tears came to my eyes and I was unable to produce a sound. Mr Frumkin shook his head.

"Let him play while we talk business."

Father looked crestfallen.

"Go and play then!" he said morosely. Then he turned to Mr Frumkin and said, "Let's get to business. I've got lots to talk over with you."

I roamed sulkily over the yard. For a while I played with a rusted motor-cycle that lay disconsolately in a corner. With all my strength I heaved it up and, leaning it against the fence, sat on the stiff, springy seat.

I examined the great mountains of bottles stacked according to their shapes and I was suddenly reminded of old Hirsh, the only bottle merchant I had ever known well. Idly I remembered his shed filled with bottles and bags and I wondered if Father would wear a shiny, brass badge as old Hirsh had.

I was recalled from my reverie by Father's shouts. We were to drive to a horse bazaar in Mr Frumkin's jinker. Sitting next to Father in the driver's seat I strained my ears to listen to Mr Frumkin who talked as if to the horse.

Father was anxious to get a handsome but tractable horse, used to city streets. His only experience of horses had been on bush roads and tracks. And Mr Frumkin kept urging Father to leave everything to him.

"Great thieves," was Mr Frumkin's description of all horse-dealers. "But leave them to me," he said, "I know them inside out. I'll pick the right horse for you. One used to the streets." He squinted knowingly at Father. "I know how to handle the thieves."

We were in the city and Father's eyes were wandering over the street; he didn't seem to be listening any longer to Mr Frumkin's wheedling talk. I too was seeing the city for the first time. I had never seen such droves of people in holiday clothes; the men in hard bowler hats and high white collars and the women in skirts that swept the dust. The street seemed to groan with the tramp of feet. Trams and motor-cars clattered by, wagons, jinkers, buggies, and carriages drawn by horses of every colour passed so close to us that I was tempted to put out my hand and brush the swiftly turning wheels. I stood up and Father clutched at my coat. "Now then," he roared into the chilly wind, and I knew that Father was really back. He was not to be trifled with just now, for I felt that he had not yet forgiven me for failing him at the bottle-yard.

Soon we reached the horse bazaar. In the street stood empty carts and drays, their shafts stuck high in the air or resting on the uneven cobblestones. Here and there a horse whinnied. In a near-by street traders sold fruit set out in long rows. Behind them children ran about in groups playing with skipping ropes and footballs made of papers. I stared at the unharnessed horses tied to posts until Mr Frumkin led us along a narrow sawdust corridor to the ring of the horse bazaar. Tier upon tier of wooden benches surrounded the sawdust-strewn, earthed arena. A pungent smell of horse sweat and fresh dung rose before us.

We clambered to the third tier of wooden benches to reach a little group of men, all acquaintances of Mr Frumkin. He introduced Father.

"Welcome to our ranks," said one of them expansively.

"Watch out that Frumkin doesn't sell you one of his good horses," said another good-humouredly. "He pretends to do you a favour but if you get in you'll never get out of his clutches."

The speaker was younger than the others. A broad-shouldered man with black, shiny curls and moustache, and restlessly roving eyes, he fixed his gaze on Father.

"Did you dream of buying horses before you came to this golden land?" he asked.

Father smiled, but the frown lining his forehead came and went so that I knew something was worrying him.

"What if I didn't?" he replied. "I haven't got an alternative now. As I find it, so I am."

"A real philosopher!" The younger man laughed.

"One must be a philosopher to make a living," replied Father.

"Take no notice of Sussman," interjected Mr Frumkin impatiently. "He'll waste your time with his philosophy. He doesn't know what he wants and he wants others to be like him."

Mr Sussman winked cynically at Father. His swarthy face wrinkled into a smile and he mimicked Mr Frumkin's slow, wheedling voice.

"Frumkin sells an old draught-horse for a racehorse to a blind man and thinks he has achieved something."

Mr Frumkin's eyes were smiling but by his voice and the quiver of his lower lip I imagined that he was very angry. His retort was lost in the clamour that sprang up round us.

The auctioneer was standing on his platform in the middle of the ring. A horse that shone like a new two-shilling piece was being slowly led around. Everything glittered with polish from its ornamental bridle to its black, well-rubbed hooves.

"What am I offered?" shouted the auctioneer and he outlined in glowing terms the virtues of the horse.

"What about him?" said Father enthusiastically.

Mr Frumkin slowly shook his head.

"He's got looks. But he doesn't like to work. He's good only for a rich spinster."

Horse after horse passed into the ring and out again, but Mr Frumkin found fault with them all, until Father said, "My luck. There are hundreds of horses here but God hasn't created one to suit me."

"Wait, there's no hurry," replied Mr Frumkin.

Then a snorting, plunging chestnut entered the ring and Mr Frumkin, out of the side of his mouth said to Father, 'There's a good horse for you. As strong as a lion."

A low cloud of thick dust hung in the air. Bids were shouted from every direction. I became excited at the sight of the chestnut who reared his head so contemptuously and I secretly hoped that Father would buy this horse. Mr Sussman however shook his head. The nostrils of his high, hooked nose quivered with distaste. He bent his head towards Father and whispered, "That's one of Frumkin's horses. A menace in a bottle-cart."

Father regretfully passed over another handsome horse but he looked at Mr Sussman with a grateful smile. His head turned away from the ring, he and Mr Sussman held a private conversation as if the noise and hustle all around were of no concern to them.

They talked of the bottle business and Mr Sussman said it was like any other business. If you could remain independent of the dealers it was good, but if you were dependent on the Frumkins it was bad.

Mr Sussman was very concerned about the fate of his old parents who still lived in the old country. It transpired that Mr Sussman came from a township close to where Father was born. They were almost second cousins, Father exclaimed affectionately and I could see that he had taken his new-found friend to his heart. What should he do, asked Mr Sussman, go back or bring his parents here?

"I must make up my mind. I believe there's a war coming," he added.

"Between whom?" Father asked sceptically.

"Everybody. The Kaiser and the Czar to start with."

"A plague on both their houses," said Father airily.

At that moment their attention was diverted by a piebald mare that stepped trippingly into the ring, like a fastidious girl.

"Pretty as a picture," said Father.

With an expression of disdain on his face, Mr Frumkin said, without turning to Father, "A harlot. Look at the way she trips around. What a life she'd lead you!"

It was nearly lunch-time when Mr Frumkin finally bought a horse for Father. A high white gelding flecked with grey, it stood patiently in its stall, its head drooped. It gazed resignedly at the empty feed box as Father gingerly patted its rump.

"Just what you want," said Mr Frumkin, "and cheap at the price."

I was bitterly disappointed. After all the frisky, high-spirited animals we had seen this white horse seemed a staid old grandfather horse. For all that, I stared for a long time at the way it stood on three legs, resting the other gracefully on the tip of its hoof. It stood like that until it was led out to the road and tied to Mr Frumkin's jinker.

Before we drove off Mr Sussman took the horse by the upper lip, looked at its teeth and ran his strong fingers over its body and then turned to its legs. He felt the knee joints, tapped the tendons, and squeezed the bone above the fetlocks.

We were already in the jinker when Mr Sussman looked up from the horse.

"A slight blemish in the legs," he said ironically. "It's one of your horses, isn't it, Frumkin? So you're going to palm it off on your good friend?"

Father and Mr Frumkin jumped off the jinker and at once held an agitated consultation. They argued, gesticulating all the time, but many of their words were lost in the wind that blew from beyond the horizon at the end of the street.

"Why didn't you tell me you had a horse for me, back at the yard?" I heard father say. "Why did we have to go through this comedy?"

Righteously Mr Frumkin said, " I gave you a chance to choose the horse you wanted."

Despite Father's vehemence I knew the horse would remain with us. From the harried expression on his face I could see that Father was in a dilemma. He was torn between a desire to get the business over and the shame of being tricked. And I suppose Mr Frumkin had lent him the money to buy this blemished horse.

Mr Frumkin kept assuring Father in a passionate voice that he had acted in his best interests. But Father's voice continued to rise until at last Mr Frumkin said pleadingly, 'Don't excite yourself. Take it for less."

"I'll take it," Father said suddenly in a resigned voice and averted his eyes from the smiling Mr Sussman. But he remained angrily silent on the journey home in Mr Frumkin's jinker.

His new business had started badly. He was in Frumkin's clutches, the horse wasn't any good, nothing would go right for him in the new land. He whispered to me that I was to say nothing to Mother about how Mr Frumkin had sold him one of his horses.

So it came about that Father was a bottle dealer, officially a licensed marine dealer. On payment of a small fee he was legally permitted to go from house to house buying empty bottles and he wore a shiny brass badge on his arm.

Mother smiled ironically at his appearance and the strong smell of horses and bottles that now clung to him. His waxed red moustache drooped and bits of chaff often stuck in his short-cropped, light-brown hair. It was terribly hard now for Father to look well-groomed and dignified.

I revelled in Father's new occupation. On every possible occasion I went with him, sometimes early in the morning before school began. With him in the streets and back lanes I met the bottle-ohs, the wood men and the rubbish collectors. Some of them had their boys to help them but Father preferred me to sit on the cart when he went into the back-yards. I seemed to embarrass him in front of his customers.

# BIG EVENTS

On the bottle-round we often met Mr Sussman driving his spring-cart. Invariably he pointed his whip at our white horse that Mr Frumkin had sold Father at the horse auction and made the same joke, "I see his legs still hold him up."

And then he would shake his head mournfully, his olive face twisting into a humorous smile.

Father flared up angrily.

"He's a good-looking horse. All right, his legs are not so good. Mine aren't either. The devil take horses and men with good legs."

For all these exchanges Father was very fond of Mr Sussman. So was Mother, and almost every Sunday he came to our house.

Sunday afternoon was our time for entertaining. After lunch we sat round waiting for our guests as though half afraid they might not come. Only after the first knock sounded hollowly down the long passage did Mother feel that our community was still about us. And her face lit up at the arrival of the first guest. Even Mr Frumkin who was sometimes among the visitors was sure of a warm welcome from her if he happened to arrive first. But we always waited with special eagerness for Mr Sussman's cheerful knock.

When he came I could see from the expectant way Father looked up that he was hoping Mr Sussman had brought the book of stories that had caused such wild laughter the previous Sunday. He was disappointed, but Mr Sussman made up for it in other ways. Mr Sussman was the leading light in the newly formed dramatic circle in the community and was by way of being a good mimic. Comic roles were his favourites and he entertained us with sketches of various bottle dealers, particularly Mr Frumkin, whom he could take off to a T.

As Mother put cakes and tea on the table Mr Sussman was mimicking the president of the Philanthropic Society, the leading notable in the community, who had come as an immigrant to this country some twenty years before. Striding round the room with his head bent low, his hands firmly clasped behind his back, he clucked with his tongue and mumbled in a strange, foreign-sounding English.

"Ah, you foreigners, how will I ever civilize you! Ah, you will be my death yet!"

Father's eyes filled with tears as he unbuttoned his vest and sat back in his chair, a glass of tea balanced precariously on his trembling palm, letting out such yells of laughter that even Mother began to laugh as I had never seen her laugh before. Then Mr Sussman jumped on a chair and began to make a speech such as notables make at a fashionable wedding of aristocrats in our community.

In the middle of this performance another knock came on the door and Miss Fanny Cohen entered. She was an acquaintance of Mother's and a regular visitor to our house. As far as I could judge she seemed older than Mother. Perhaps that was because she had a feathery down on her upper lip and along the sides of her face. And besides, she was always dressed as if in perpetual mourning.

At the sight of Mr Sussman hot blood surged into her face. Muttering her greetings she sat down quickly on the sofa in the far corner and, producing her crocheting, bent her head over an unfinished scarf. Her face still flushed, she stealthily glanced from beneath heavy eyelids at the merry faces round and then deliberately sent the ball of wool rolling from her knees. She bent down and fumbled with her fingers over the floor.

Father roguishly wagged a finger at her, "Always blushing!"

"Please," Mother intervened. "You and your clumsy male humour."

"Now what have I done," Father said, turning up the palms of his hands in bewilderment. His face wore an expression of childish innocence and his pale-blue eyes roamed over the room.

"You have done nothing," Miss Cohen came hastily to his aid. Gabbling her words she turned towards Mr Sussman, "Please go on with your stories, Mr Sussman. Why must you stop because I have come in?"

But Mr Sussman's animation died away. He told us one more story of a horse he knew that could only understand Yiddish, not a word of English, and then the conversation turned to news from abroad, to the newest arrivals, to tittle-tattle, and the war that Mr Sussman said was coming. Miss Cohen crocheted in silence until the party broke up.

Father was still fretting from Mother's rebuke and as soon as our guests left an irritable conversation began. Why was Father so clumsy? demanded Mother. Couldn't he see that poor Fanny Cohen's heart was bursting for Sussman? Such a refined, intelligent woman who had been a student in Russia. What a pity she had been left on the shelf! And Father had only probed at her wound.

As he listened Father's blue eyes glistened with anger, and finally he roared petulantly, "How am I to know what is going on in an old girl's heart?"

Mother replied, coaxingly for once, "Just so. But I always thought you did know what was going on in a human heart."

He glanced round aimlessly and I could see that he was softening. Rubbing his chin, he pouted his lips as if assailed by a sudden thought.

"Perhaps it would be a good thing," he said, "for both of them if we could bring them together. Sometimes people need a little outside assistance."

So, some time later, when Father and I were seated beside Mr Sussman in the driver's seat of his wagonette Father nudged him and nodded his head in the direction of Miss Cohen who was waiting patiently at the gate of our house for Mother.

"A fine woman. Intelligent and good-looking," Father said with an air of an authority on such matters.

"Yes, a fine woman," Mr Sussman answered almost un-willingly and his dark eyes were fixed on the two horses with ribbons in their collars in honour of the occasion of our picnic.

Mother came presently and she and my sister sat in the back seat with Miss Cohen. We drove off towards the hills. I could hardly restrain a shout as Mr Sussman urged on the two horses down the straight flat road outside the city. The warm sun caressed our faces and Father took a deep breath, smiling back at Mother.

"A great pleasure," he said simply, and even Mother seemed to be enjoying the surroundings. She gazed at the wisps of feathery white clouds that floated in the high ex-panse of blue sky. A gentle breeze laden with fresh spring scents blew from the hills that loomed before us.

We moved up the gravel road towards the hills through country patterned with the browns of ploughed paddocks and the greens of young crops. Then, climbing all the time until the horses began to sweat and a yellowish foam appeared on their quivering hides, we reached the top of a ridge and it was suddenly a different world.

"A remarkable country!" exclaimed Father to Mr Sussman. "Here you have hills. Down there they grow everything, somewhere else sand. They even have snow, I've been told."

Far off were row upon row of black and blue hills and on one side of the road the valley rolled down towards a river that coursed its way through narrow channels overlooked by gaunt trees.

We stopped at a picnic ground guarded by rows of pine trees. The sun was shining through the trees and away off we could see the city rising near the sea. Mr Sussman tied the horses to a pine-tree and hung nosebags over their ears Miss Cohen was helping Mother to unpack a hamper and she constantly turned her gaze in the direction of Mr Sussman. There was no doubt that he was remarkable in everything. The way he handled those two horses brought words of admiration from Father, who stood near Mother and Miss Cohen.

"What a talent for everything the man has!" Father said enthusiastically, and he stared quizzically at Miss Cohen "And with all that he has such a strong character. And he tells such good jokes," he added, shifting his gaze to Mother who nodded her head in agreement.

Shortly after we had finished lunch, which had stretched well into the afternoon, Mr Sussman restlessly suggested that we all climb a high hill beyond the picnic ground, from where we could see for great distances. But Father, who lay sprawled on the grass sucking his pipe, rubbed his stomach and shook his head. He said he was too old and weary for mountain climbing, but it would be quite all right if the young people left him and Mother here while they went on their ramble.

Miss Cohen suddenly laughed with a grating, nervous laugh.

"It wouldn't be nice to break up the company," she said.

She looked round expectantly, first at Mother and then at Mr Sussman but he merely said, "Well, let it be."

I kept hovering round the group, the ladies sitting facing the men. Miss Cohen seemed unnaturally full of high spirits and laughed more than was necessary. But Father and Mr Sussman were so absorbed in each other's words that they seemed unaware of anyone else. Slowly a frown gathered on Mother's face and imperceptibly the distance between the ladies and the men grew.

Two separate conversations sprang up. Mother and Miss Cohen talked with pathos of the life they had left behind; here everything was so different from what they had known before—even the sky, the trees, the very earth.

Mr Sussman grew wistful about the hills. He was born in the shadow of snow-capped mountains and he had not given up hope of seeing them again. In a whisper he confided that if war broke out as some people said it would, he would be tempted to go abroad if only to see his old home. He had often thought of bringing his parents here, but he felt they were too old to accustom themselves to new and bewildering surroundings. He, Mr Sussman, had never been able to settle down here. On the other hand, with the little money he had made, he could live in comfort with his parents over there. But when he had to make up his mind he became irresolute.

Father glanced anxiously in the direction of Mother and said quietly, "Make up your mind quickly. Take my advice Sussman, don't live in two worlds! My wife does. But it's no good."

"Perhaps a war will decide for me," Mr Sussman answered seriously.

Soon after the picnic I was vividly reminded of Mr Sussman's talk about a coming war. It was at the shipping office where Mother had taken me to act as her interpreter.

We were no sooner in the handsome office than she hurried towards a clerk who was familiar to us, so often had Mother been here before. He spoke loudly and repeated his words over and over again, as though we were deaf. There were rumours that travelling would soon be very difficult and much more expensive and unless Mother booked immediately she might not be able to go for quite a long while. Mother stared incredulously at the clerk, who stared back at us with happy, unconcerned eyes.

Mother took leave of the office with such an anxious expression on her face that I was afraid to speak a word to her. She hastened home to speak to Father. We must decide; it was now or perhaps never. We must buy tickets on the cheapest line and go, even if it meant we should arrive penniless over there.

So Mother argued, but Father wouldn't hear of it. We must wait patiently, he said. Perhaps the war would never come or even if it did it might only last a few months.

"Then we'll see," he concluded.

"What do you mean?" Mother almost groaned, looking fearfully at Father. Her gaze, like that of one caught in a trap, was just the same as when we left the shipping office.

"I mean we can't go for a while yet. It is impossible. We haven't got the money. And even if we had enough for tickets who would feed us when we got there?" Father answered calmly.

"You want to stay here, I know. You will use every excuse," Mother said unreasonably.

And stay we did. The war came and shattered Mother's hopes, and when Mr Sussman announced he was joining the army she gave vent to her bitterness by arguing vehemently with him.

"Why do you have to give your life for the Russian Czar and his cousin the English King?" she asked. "What have they done for you? Leave them to fight their other cousin, the Kaiser, and may they all break their heads."

Mr Sussman found it hard to explain why he was so anxious to join the army. His customary eloquence deserted him; his nimble tongue seemed sticking to the roof of his mouth. He glanced round the room, a frown furrowing his swarthy face and the nostrils of his high, hooked nose quivered nervously. From the far corner of the room Miss Fanny Cohen looked into his face intently. She was dressed in deep black as always and a light tremor shook her huddled body.

"I must go like the others. Am I any different from them?" he suddenly burst out miserably.

With an impatient shrug of her narrow, stooped shoulders Mother went into the kitchen. From there she called, "I thought you were a resolute man. But you have no mind of your own."

Just then Miss Cohen got up and without saying a word walked towards the corridor. Beads of perspiration shone on her hairy lip and her eyes were dim.

She ran down the corridor and went out. Father and Mr Sussman jumped up from their seats and Mother hurried in from the kitchen.

"What has happened?" she cried.

"Fanny has gone," Father said in a bewildered voice.

Mother glanced at Mr Sussman who, with unseeing eyes was staring at the chair in the corner. As if painfully thinking of something, his lips were moving; he looked anything but a soldier to me.

"Run after her and bring her back," Mother called to me.

Outside, a squally wind brought the smell of rain. There was a snatch of sun and then spits of rain as I ran down the deserted street. Overhead the clouds were flying fast. As I came up to Miss Cohen she attempted to compose herself. But she avoided my glance and her face was faintly streaked with crimson.

"Mother wants you to come back," I said.

"Not now, my dear," she answered. "Later." Her voice trailed off to a whisper.

I stood and watched her run blindly. Stumbling over the hem of her skirt she ran across the uneven stones of the road. Then she disappeared from my sight.

As soon as I returned home Mother asked, "Why didn't you bring her back, you foolish boy?" And without waiting to hear from me she said, "I shall go and get her myself."

Walking round the room she muttered to herself, "All of us run like frightened mice," and Father and Mr Sussman stared at her with dull eyes. She seemed to be looking for something and then, suddenly seizing her coat, she left the house.

Father sat watching Mr Sussman but neither made a sound. The gleaming red point of Mr Sussman's cigarette shone in the darkening room. Outside clouds had hidden the sky and a fine rain was falling. Father shook himself suddenly, blew his nose noisily, and said in an impatient voice, "What are you running away from? I know you're not going because you want to serve the King. You're just running away. You think you will solve something? You'll have to come back after the war."

"Maybe," said Mr Sussman.

And before he could say another word, Father interposed with, "What 'maybe' is there about it? You won't belong over there any more."

Then Father added, "We belong to this new earth. It has sucked us in whether we know it or not."

# SISTERS

CAME the cold, rainy winter bringing silent, dimly-lit streets and I spent every night at home furtively reading boys' papers and pink sporting sheets.

Mother was in the best room entertaining four ladies and although their voices floated out into the kitchen I was deaf to them. Even Father's voice emerging from behind a newspaper couldn't make itself heard against the maze of thoughts that filled my head.

"Deaf whenever your father talks, eh?" he shouted into my ear.

Snatching the magazine out of my hands he glared at the crude drawing of a man with a revolver on the cover, grimaced with distaste and said, "Wonderful books you read! If your mother catches you with this piffle you'll not hear the end of it and you'll deserve it."

Father sat beside me in front of the stove, his feet on the edge of the open oven. Thoughtfully he turned the magazine in his hands and with a glance in the direction of Mother's room he said, "I'll give it back to you if you read the newspaper to me. But quickly, for certainly Mother will soon come and ask me to talk to the ladies."

Father always asked me to read the paper to him but never without some fuss. Even now as he handed me the evening newspaper he grumbled, "Don't imagine you are doing me a favour. Your father isn't an illiterate. He can read in more languages than you can even imagine."

Somehow it cost him his health to reach the point of asking me to read to him, for he had already painfully scanned the headlines, coughed loudly and muttered to himself before giving up.

But as I read he forgot his pride, stretched his feet comfortably into the oven and settled down as if at a performance of a revue or comedy, to marvel and to criticize. He applauded a speech or shook his head vigorously in disagreement with some report or laughed uproariously at what he thought was outlandish or far-fetched. Every now and again he turned to the door and sighed.

"Just as I'm getting into the paper Mother's sure to want me to go into the room with the old girls," he interrupted my reading.

So when Mother came into the kitchen to make supper for her guests, Father looked up at her as though she were a mortal enemy. He said resentfully, "I suppose I must go and say good evening to the ladies."

"Yes," Mother replied. "And don't forget to tie your bootlaces," she added as she filled the kettle and placed it on the stove.

I followed Father in to the best room; it was called the dining-room, though we never had our meals there. Our best furniture was in this room, a horsehair sofa, a table with a red plush cover with golden tassels, and six chairs with cane backs.

Father greeted cheerfully the four ladies seated on the chairs under enlarged photographs of my grandparents. My grandparents looked sad and so did the ladies. They were sisters and Father secretly spoke of them not by their names but as the old one, the fat one, the middle pin, and the youngster.

They were all rather stout and all had undershot, jutting jaws. All wore thick glasses, for they were short-sighted, and they all dressed in the same style. They wore dark jackets and skirts as though in mourning. Because they were serious women and were always doing something for the cultural life of our community Mother thought very well of them and often invited them to the house.

The old one, Miss Liza, taught the violin and Mother was anxiously considering whether my sister or I should start taking lessons from her.

My sister had been in the room all the time and she ran up to Father who was staring at the ladies, not knowing what he should do next. She whispered loudly that she would like to take lessons from Miss Liza.

'Please, Daddy, do let me."

I sniggered approvingly at her, for I was not at all anxious to spend my free time on the fiddle. Father asked Miss Liza what she thought of the girl as a likely player.

"Who can tell?" replied Miss Liza in a voice of a doctor reluctant to pronounce the fateful verdict.

"What do you mean, who can tell?" Father asked belligerently. "You just take a look at her hands. Beautiful. A real fiddler's hands. That must mean something, surely," he added with certainty.

My sister held out her hands and Miss Liza and her sisters involuntarily gazed at them.

'What can hands tell?" Miss Liza said. "It is the heart that speaks through a violin."

"It is the heart," echoed the fat one.

"Some virtuosi have stumpy fingers but they make divine music," chimed the middle pin.

The youngster remained silent, gazing at Father with affected sorrow.

"What's all this talk of the heart?" Father argued persistently. "First you must learn to play with the hands, surely?" he went on.

The four sisters looked at him pityingly and two fiery spots appeared on Father's cheekbones.

There was an uncomfortable silence until Mother came in with a tray laden with cups, a plate of cakes, a steaming kettle, and the tea in a strainer. She guessed that words had passed between the ladies and Father, for on other occasions he had tried to dispute with them. She knew there was always a kind of resentment in his manner when he was in the company of the sisters.

Mother looked intently at him and said in a kindly voice, "Why don't you sit down?"

Awkwardly Father walked to the end of the room and sat down on the sofa. It seemed to me that his head, shoulders, and arms made angry shadows on the blind at the window behind him. Our long-stemmed lamp in the middle of the table and the candles on the mantelpiece cast haloes of light over the heads of the ladies while Father sat in a pocket of darkness.

Turning their backs on him, the ladies drank cups of tea and with cocked heads listened to Mother as she talked of my sister and the violin. There was a note of doubt in her voice as she turned to Miss Liza and asked was not the fiddle really a more suitable instrument for a boy than a girl.

"After all, one rarely hears of a girl virtuoso," she added.

Miss Liza sniffed audibly and I am sure I heard her sisters sniff one after the other in a descending scale.

"What opportunity have girls ever had to be virtuosi?" Miss Liza demanded.

"Have men ever encouraged women to be anything but drudges and servants?" said the fat one in a petulant tone.

"It's a man's world, more's the pity," sighed the middle pin.

The youngster still remained silent but she looked round with a superior expression at Father wrapped in gloom on the sofa.

Mother suddenly became apologetic.

"You are quite right, Miss Liza," she said humbly. "Girls have never been given a chance."

"And when they do get a chance," Miss Liza went on, pressing home her victory, "they will most certainly surpass men."

"This man's world won't last for ever," said the middle pin. "Women are not bending the knee as they did once," she concluded with a snort.

"I should think not," said the fat one and burst into a short, grating laugh.

From the sofa came Father's irritable, loud voice. It was as though he were about to make a last desperate stand for something or other. "Tell me what you women will do when you wear the trousers and we go into skirts? Answer that one," he said boldly.

"So you really think we couldn't answer that question?" replied Miss Liza in a mocking tone, shaking her head energetically and pursing her lips with contempt.

"Ha, ha, ha," chorused her sisters.

Miss Liza took up the attack.

"Just like a man's impertinence to think he can ask one question and dispose of everything," she said.

She would have gone on, but Mother interrupted her.

"We seem to have gone a long way from the subject of the violin," she said in a soothing voice, addressing the four sisters and glancing out of the corner of her eye at Father.

"There will be time enough for argument," she added,

as though to appease the sisters who might regard her, God forbid, as a weakling, a mere nothing in the hands of a man.

"Very well," said Miss Liza with emphasis, "but I can assure you I am always happy to argue with any man."

"Of course I understand," said Mother gravely, "but, Miss Liza, let us make some arrangement about the lessons. When can my girl come to you? Or would you prefer to come here?"

Before Miss Liza could make a reply Father, who had been fretfully chewing one end of his moustache boomed triumphantly, "And who is going to pay for the lessons? And who is going to buy the fiddle?"

Mother stared at him with a pained expression. Then, to hide her embarrassment, she stood up from the chair and, averting her eyes from the ladies, walked over to the table and began to fill the cups with tea again.

"Well, who is?" Father spoke his words jauntily and a smile broke over his face.

"Well, well," said Miss Liza. "Who ever spoke of money? Did I? Did you?" she said to her sisters with affected innocence. "I intend to teach her without money and I intend to lend her a violin. I hope that will be satisfactory to all," she said ironically, glancing at Father.

Then she rose from her chair, followed by her sisters and they all said together, "We must go now. Don't trouble yourself with more tea."

Politely they nodded to Father and wished him a good night. Then, led by Miss Liza they made for the door. There was an expression of satisfaction and triumph on their faces as they disappeared into the passage. Mother hurried after them and we could hear subdued voices at the front door.

When Mother returned Father looked at her with astonished eyes.

"Who could have thought it?" he said. "I suppose I should have said something, but what could I say? They really didn't talk of money, did they?"

Father spoke sheepishly but I knew he wanted to say something devastating about the ladies, something that would repair his damaged self-esteem.

"You know," he said in an easy, confidential voice, "I'm not surprised those old girls were never snatched off the shelf. First, they're always together. Then they go about looking for fights. A man would have to be a boxer to marry one of them. The youngster must be the worst; she never opens her mouth. But can you imagine what she thinks? It must be terrible."

"They're very fine women," Mother said quietly, "and I wish you would stop calling them the old girls."

"Well, they're not a bunch of youngsters," Father said, smiling.

"Neither are we youngsters," said Mother and she looked strangely at him.

His smile disappeared.

"Don't misunderstand me," he said. "They're old maids. And no great beauties either," he floundered on. "And a joke won't do them any harm."

Mother replied tartly, "I've said before I don't appreciate your humour. Isn't an old maid a human being to you?"

"All right!" Father said impatiently and, rising heavily from the sofa, he stamped his feet on the floor as though to break the floor-boards.

"Come and read the paper," he pointed his thumb peremptorily at me.

Then muttering to himself he went back to the kitchen and I dutifully followed him.

# UNCLE ISAAC

My sister and I once spent a year away from home. It was when Mother was sick in hospital and convalescent home and Father was working in the country. Our bits of furniture were stored and we were boarded with a middle-aged childless couple some streets from where we lived.

We called the pair "uncle" and "auntie" and in some remote way they were related to us on our mother's side. Uncle Isaac was a little, fat man with a remarkable fund of odd bits of information. Any sort of conversation was an invitation for him to bring forth his knowledge. If Auntie Fanny mentioned the price of fish he would ask us if we knew that sharks had more than one set of teeth.

Uncle Isaac was always busy. He was for ever absorbed in his business in the city and he rarely spent much time in the house. But every evening after tea he spent a while in the dining-room. He would produce a ledger book and with great rapidity enter figures, adding and subtracting out loud. Finished, he went to the mirror on the wall, stared at himself for a brief moment, arranged his tie, patted his fat cheeks, smoothed his grey, curly hair, and said in a serious voice, "Isaac, you must rest now."

Turning to me he said, "In Spain they have siestas after lunch, I have mine after tea. Do you know why they have siestas in Spain?"

I can't remember just why they have siestas in Spain but Uncle Isaac certainly told me. His own siesta was a hurried one. He lay down for barely a quarter of an hour and when he opened his eyes he stretched himself with pleasure, rose from the sofa and said, "Now I'm as fresh and lively as a two-year-old."

And out he went again. I was never sure whether he was going on business or to visit friends. He was not like any other head of a household I had ever known, he was like a boarder in the house.

Auntie Fanny lived her own life, never commenting on her husband's whirlwind comings and goings. Just as he was always in a hurry with only time to spare for imparting bits of information, she was always slow and measured in her movements and as grave and orderly as a religious service. Apart from her housework, over which she spent hours every day so that every floor shone with polish and every doorknob gleamed, Auntie Fanny daily sat in her rocking chair and crocheted baby clothes for this woman or that in the neighbourhood.

There was a time and place for everything in her house. We rose at the same hour every morning, we ate our meals at the same time every day. The merest trifle had its own place. There were cupboards for this and that, racks and shelves everywhere; it was maddening for my sister and me. And Uncle Isaac sympathized with us and he said that if there were children in the house all the time this order would never last.

The sabbath was an awesome day for us. Auntie Fanny was a very pious lady and she never allowed us out of her sight on this day. She was afraid Uncle Isaac wanted to entice me out of her hands and take me to the city. He sinned by driving his sulky on the sabbath but she was determined to make sure I did not share in his sin.

After synagogue and lunch, when Uncle Isaac disappeared from the house, Auntie Fanny read to us from her favourite parts of the Bible; the story of the captivity of the Jews in Egypt and the story of her favourite prophet, Jeremiah. Only at sunset did she let us go out of the house for a short stroll in the street.

Our evening meal over, Auntie Fanny entertained guests in the sitting-room. There was Madame Koch, the retired midwife, a retinue of old ladies, and a widow or two. I was never allowed into the company and I was even afraid to put my ear to the keyhole. There seemed something mysterious and frightening about the conversation within. Rare words occasionally did penetrate the door and wall. They were about births, and deaths, about deceased parents and the vanished past.

Once Uncle Issac came home unexpectedly and took me and my sister into the sitting-room. He wanted to show us off in front of the ladies. And I daresay he wanted them to see how well cared for we were, so that the news could be spread through the community.

But Uncle Isaac took one look round the room and whispered to me so that all could hear, "A cheerful assembly, eh?"

An old lady looked up sharply and said ironically, "Perhaps if you joined us you would make things more lively."

"Nothing I could say would make you any more cheerful," he replied gravely.

I could see that Uncle Isaac was no favourite in this company. Then one of the women, without looking in his direction, said sneeringly, "I'm sure it wouldn't do the menfolk any harm if they spent a little more time with their wives."

"If I had a family perhaps I'd take your advice," said Uncle Isaac weakly.

He suddenly went red in the face at his own words. From his expression I was sure he would have gladly bitten off his tongue. He hurried us out of the room without speaking another word.

It was not long after this that I overheard a strange conversation between Uncle Isaac and Auntie Fanny. They were whispering together in the kitchen and the words that floated through the half-closed door that separated me from them made me listen intently.

"The beginning of December I think. I saw the midwife, Mrs Mendelsohn, today," Auntie Fanny said.

Her voice was agitated and Uncle Isaac coughed nervously. But they talked no more about the matter. Soon Uncle Isaac came out of the kitchen and sat down in his chair at the head of the round polished table. I could see he wanted to say something to me but the words were slow in coming. This was so different from usual when words flowed from his mouth. His eyes roamed round the room from the polished candlesticks on the mantelpiece to the tapestry on the wall. Without looking at me he picked up a newspaper and pretended to read.

But soon the newspaper fell from his hands and he blew his nose impatiently. With an embarrassed smile on his face he drummed his fingers on the table and said, "You'll have to be very good to Auntie Fanny now. You must do everything she says and you must never annoy her."

I stared at him in astonishment for he had never spoken to me like this before. He had never shown any interest in our everyday behaviour and I did not think Auntie Fanny had ever spoken to him about us. I nodded my head as he continued to talk about how we should conduct ourselves, irrationally repeating his words over and over again, and it seemed to me that he was really filled with an impulse to unburden his heart but he just didn't know how. For once he didn't produce his ledger, nor did he leave the house as was his custom.

From that evening onwards a great change came over Uncle Isaac. There were whole days when he stayed at home. He would drive away to his shop in the city and then return as though he had remembered something important. His yellow sulky standing before the front gate became a familiar sight in our street. His grey horse would stand patiently, a nosebag over its ears, waiting for the evening when Uncle Isaac would drive him away to the stable in the lane behind the house.

Auntie Fanny had withdrawn into herself. We rarely heard more than a few words from her and from morning till night she crocheted baby clothes. She had lost interest in her housework and now she never reprimanded us for disturbing the tidy arrangement of things in the bathroom. Uncle Isaac often urged her to walk in the street with him but she invariably refused.

"Why this interest?" she said to him. "You never asked me to go out before."

He pretended he hadn't heard her and noisily and clumsily pottered about in the kitchen. He wiped a few dishes, put them on the wrong shelves, rolled the wet dish-cloth into a ball and threw it into a corner of the room. Then he darted into another room looking for something new to do. He found a geography book that I had brought home from school and for a few minutes became immersed

in the pictures of cities and maps of countries. He had discovered some new facts and promptly related them to Auntie
Fanny who never lifted her eyes from her crocheting. All
the time he looked at her with an expression of anxious
interest.

Suddenly she said, "Have you nothing to do outside?"

"Don't you want my help?" he answered in a hurt voice.
"Then I shall go."

He left the house but he soon came back. Nothing would
keep him away and just as once he rarely stayed in the
house, now he never wanted to leave it.

Auntie Fanny was often sick and in pain. There were
days when she could hardly walk owing to the tormenting
pains in her legs and she tottered about dragging her feet
one behind the other. She bore her pain silently and it
never found any reflection in her face. Even when beads of
sweat stood out on her temples, when the pain was intense,
her eyes still glowed warmly. But Uncle Isaac could not
see her suffering in silence. His voice rose in vexation:

"Please let me call Dr McDiarmid. Everyone speaks well
of him. What does a midwife know?"

Auntie Fanny obstinately refused to have Dr McDiarmid
in the house. She was quite content with Mrs Mendelsohn
who was well spoken of by the ladies of the community.

Mrs Mendelsohn had a large family of her own and when
she visited the house she always brought her two youngest
in a black-hooded perambulator that she left on the veranda.
Auntie Fanny always took her into the best room and
danced attendance upon her as though she were the patient.
She made her cups of tea and baked a cake in honour of
her coming. Mrs Mendelsohn ate heartily and talked loudly

and never let Auntie Fanny ask those questions that troubled her.

"What's a bit of pain?" said Mrs Mendelsohn as though anticipating Auntie Fanny's thoughts. "I often say our grandmothers had a worse time and they survived and here we are today."

Uncle Isaac was very uneasy about the midwife. He had his mind fixed on Dr McDiarmid and he began to think that Mrs Mendelsohn was in some way responsible for his wife's poor health.

One day as Mrs Mendelsohn was about to wheel her large black-hooded perambulator off the veranda, Uncle Isaac approached her with a dignified expression and suggested that she call in the doctor. He had read somewhere that new methods had recently been discovered and he was sure that so worthy a doctor as the Scotsman McDiarmid would be familiar with them.

Mrs Mendelsohn drew up her robust frame to her full height so that she looked down on Uncle Isaac's grey curly hair and she shot him a glance of contempt from beneath thick, black eyebrows.

"And why are you so concerned, pray?" she said. "Are you having the baby?"

"I don't know if you have ever read—" he began, but she interrupted him.

"I wish you would attend to your own affairs. And read only those books that concern you. Like books on second-hand clothes."

She placed her Gladstone bag on the hood of the pram and without another word pushed her children down the street. I knew she would never forgive Uncle Isaac for his lack of confidence.

But Uncle Isaac had got Dr McDiarmid into his mind and when he found Auntie Fanny lying down he returned to the subject.

"What does Mrs Mendelsohn know? Call in a man of science, I beg you. I can't bear to see you suffer," he pleaded.

"I don't want your learned men," Auntie Fanny burst out. "I'm satisfied with my own people. You prefer the strangers, I know," she added morosely.

His ruddy face turned pale and only with difficulty did he suppress his vexation in front of Auntie Fanny. But as soon as he ran out of the house he began to shout ugly and hateful words at the inoffensive horse who looked at him with grateful eyes.

I now spent many an hour with Uncle Isaac and even on the sabbath I occasionally drove with him to his shop in the city. The shop was in a back street and there was an iron grille over the window. There were three different locks on the front door and Uncle Isaac complained that he wasted a lot of time opening and shutting them. It was a nuisance having to come at all, though now he opened the shop infrequently. This was the Uncle Isaac who had always been absorbed in his business and who took a delight in his second-hand goods.

There was one special room of treasures he wouldn't part with, old clocks with pictures on their faces, chairs with strangely carved legs, sets and sets of different-shaped cups and saucers, a long-stemmed German pipe. They were arranged round the room as at a museum. On the wall hung a sword that Uncle Isaac said had been used in the Franco-Prussian war. It had been the proud possession of a German officer.

Uncle Isaac knew everything about his treasures and as he related fact after fact about them he would find himself digressing into the realms of science, the history of mankind or the history of clockmaking.

"Now take that brooch over there," he said, pointing to a glass-topped box, "it was made in Paris over a hundred years ago. Paris then was ruled over by a king. The brooch was made by a firm that supplied the royal family. Who can say but that brooch was not worn by the queen herself?"

The more often I came to the shop the more I learned about his treasures, right back to their genesis. Although he talked freely to me I was conscious all the time of his anxiety. It seemed to me his mind was with Auntie Fanny so that he was never able to rest in the shop. He ran from room to room, never dusted his treasures as he kept promising himself he would, and listened with impatience to the odd buyer or seller who came into the shop.

One November day we drove home in the twilight, less than two hours after Uncle Isaac had opened his shop. A blue, rose-tinted haze hung over the house as Uncle Isaac quickly unharnessed the horse, filled the bin with chaff, and hurried towards the kitchen.

We found Auntie Fanny sitting on a chair in the unlit room groaning and holding her hands beneath her stomach, while my sister stood against the wall staring wide-eyed at Auntie's writhing lips.

"What's the matter?" Uncle Isaac asked in a hoarse voice.

"Fetch Mrs Mendelsohn. Go, hurry," she whispered.

Uncle Isaac fixed dilated eyes vacantly on his wife while seconds like hours passed. Suddenly he ran out of the kitchen, stopped in the middle of the yard, turned his head and shouted to me.

"Help your auntie to her room."

She slowly shook her head.

"You can't help me," she said.

My sister and I walked behind Auntie Fanny, who almost fell at every step. The passageway was in complete darkness and I hurried back to fetch a lamp.

Holding the lamp in front of me, I peered into Auntie Fanny's room. I was frightened by the sight of her lying in her clothes on the bed, her face distorted, her wet cheek pressed against the pillow. Sweat was pouring into her sunken eyes. Auntie Fanny cast a weakly smiling glance at me and called me towards her. I was suddenly alarmed, for I thought she must surely be dying.

"Take your sister into the kitchen," she whispered. "Don't be frightened," she went on. "I'll be all right. I'm in God's hands," she added with great effort, her eyes screwed up tightly.

I clasped my sister's hand and led her from the room. She whimpered protestingly but I was carried away by Auntie Fanny's request that was like a sacred command and I almost dragged her the length of the passageway into our bedroom. I was filled with a sense of the importance of the occasion and I felt I was playing a very responsible role in the house.

From the room I heard the voices of women in the passageway. Uncle Isaac must have notified every lady in the community on his wild run for Mrs Mendelsohn, for I never saw so many of them in the house at once before. I walked back into the corridor but the women wouldn't budge to let me pass. But they all made way when through the open front door came an old shrunken woman followed by a retinue of women much like herself.

The ancient lady wore a frilly white cap like an egg white and she and her followers made for Auntie Fanny's room, opened the door and went in without speaking a word to anybody.

"That's Madame Koch and her retinue," one woman said.

Another said, "I thought she had long retired from practice."

"No one can keep her away from a confinement," added yet another.

But just then Mrs Mendelsohn, the midwife, and Uncle Isaac arrived. With a purposeful, serious expression on her round, swarthy face as though to say, "I have arrived in the nick of time," Mrs Mendelsohn turned the doorknob of Auntie's room and I caught a glimpse of the hunched shoulders of the old women hovering round the bed in the streaky, yellowish lamplight.

As the door closed Uncle Isaac turned frenziedly to the women in the dark passage and they to cheer him up began telling him of their own experiences and chiding him for his masculine weakness. I heard one woman out of Uncle's hearing whisper to another, "You can't blame him for behaving like a frightened child. By rights he should be a grandfather. But better late than never."

The other said, "She ought to be proud of her husband. Now, my man never blinked an eyelid when I had my last. He said to me, 'You know the way to the hospital. Let me rest'."

"But of course it was your sixth."

"But what has that to do with the matter?"

I no longer listened to the conversation for the door of Auntie Fanny's room opened again and out came the old women followed by Mrs Mendelsohn dressed in a spotlessly starched gown. They were all arguing loudly.

The shrunken old lady with the frilly white cap protested in a high-pitched, toothless voice against Mrs Mendelsohn's imperious ways. What right had she to cast her out of the labour room? She had been the first midwife in the community, long before Mrs Mendelsohn wore plaits. She, Madame Koch, had brought many into the world, even some of the people in this very corridor. She pointed a withered hand at several women at the front door. The retinue of old women chimed in with angry voices, Madame Koch knew more than Mrs Mendelsohn would ever know.

Mrs Mendelsohn impatiently tapped a foot on the floor and in a cold, dignified voice said, without even looking in the direction of her ancient rival, that she would have no truck with so-called midwives who practised spells and incantations. She was a real midwife with a diploma. With that Mrs Mendelsohn quickly turned her back on her angry enemies and banged the door in their faces.

The old women clustered round Madame Koch kept to themselves, refusing to stir from their place near the door. The others in the corridor moved closer to Uncle Isaac and stood near the front door and on the veranda. I sidled past the old women and joined Uncle Isaac. He seemed pleased to see me and asked me what I had done with my sister. Before I could tell him she was in bed he had turned away and was staring vacantly at the women talking animatedly round him.

One said, "Madame Koch is as often in the death chamber as the labour room now. Both places are the same to her, I should think."

"She goes to every funeral," said another.

Still another said, "These old crones shouldn't be allowed into a room where there's a new life. Preserve us from the evil eye," she continued in a mysterious voice. "Thanks be to God my children aren't here."

Uncle Isaac suddenly looked with loathing at the women with their complacent faces. As Auntie Fanny screamed again the blood drained from his face.

"I can't stand this any more," he said loudly. "She's dying in there and here I stand like a block of wood." Then he continued with passion, "We live in an age of electricity, of steamships and scientific thought and I have to listen to all these old wives' tales. The evil eye! Did you ever hear of it?"

Uncle Isaac, stirred by his own words, ran down the passage, through the back-yard towards the stable. Although I was by his side he talked to himself all the while he harnessed the horse, who stumbled sleepily as it was led into the lane.

I climbed into the sulky behind Uncle Isaac and he cracked the whip in the air and swung the reins round the horse's head. Without looking this way or that he drove fast towards the doctor's house. The horse responded to his demands as if it understood the importance of the mission and cantered over the uneven stones of the road.

After Uncle Isaac had seen Doctor McDiarmid he drove more quietly and we arrived back a minute or so before the doctor drove up to the house in his open car. The lights of the car shone on a group of men, husbands of the women inside, who stood idly near the edge of the footpath. The clatter of the car brought some of the women to the gate.

Doctor McDiarmid, a stout, red-faced man with curled, waxed moustaches, good-naturedly pushed his way through the women who crowded the path and doorway. He said cheerfully to Uncle Isaac, "Where's the patient?"

Then he asked in a puzzled voice, "What are all these people doing here?"

Uncle Isaac began to make some explanation about the different customs of people from other countries but he stopped suddenly and walked hurriedly to the door of Auntie Fanny's bedroom. He was too anxious to get the doctor to his wife to hold him up with talk.

As the doctor opened the door Madame Koch and her retinue of old women, who had been watching him with darting eyes, stepped behind him into the room from which they had been driven. Uncle Isaac looked about helplessly and for once not a sound came from his mouth. Some men who had come up to him to speak words of encouragement shrugged their shoulders and left him alone. With his pale face, his vacant eyes, and his limp arms hanging by his sides he looked more dead than alive.

It seemed that hours had passed when the door of the bedroom opened and the doctor came out, a large smile wrinkling his red face.

"Congratulations, a boy," he said to Uncle Isaac.

Uncle Isaac stared open-mouthed for a moment. Suddenly he opened wide his arms and weeping for joy kissed me wildly on the face. He shouted to the assembly of men and women, "A boy! My wife has given me a boy! Good folk, how can I repay my wife?"

He kept repeating his words until the doctor said, "You can go in and see your wife now."

Uncle Isaac was more like himself when he grasped the doorknob, but suddenly a smile of embarrassment passed over his face and he called to me, "Come in with me."

I joined him and held his burning hand as we came into the bedroom. I could just hear Auntie Fanny's quivering voice as Uncle Isaac bent down to kiss her mouth.

My eyes turned to the white and red living thing that was stirring in Madame Koch's arms. The tiny boy was passed from hand to hand, each old woman mumbling a strange-sounding blessing over him. Gradually their strange chorus rose to a rhapsody of joy. "Praise God for a new living being!" Madame Koch cried shrilly. Then, pronounced a perfect specimen, free from all blemishes, the child was delivered from the shrivelled but sure hands of the old lady into Uncle Isaac's nervous grasp. He gazed down in astonishment and admiration at the tiny mouth from which came a long wail.

Mrs Mendelsohn, the midwife, who had just finished drying her hands at a table near the head of Auntie Fanny's bed watched the scene with rising anger and finally burst out to Uncle Isaac in a loud and peremptory voice, "Give me the child. And please ask those women to leave at once."

And as an afterthought she added, "And go yourself. You have seen your wife and boy."

A shrill chorus rose against Mrs Mendelsohn as she took the child from Uncle Isaac's hands and put it beside Auntie Fanny.

"Why do you give yourself such airs?" asked Madame Koch in a sing-song voice. "You should be thankful for the assistance I gave you."

"The assistance you gave me!" Mrs Mendelsohn gasped as if unable to believe her ears.

"Yes, the assistance Madame Koch gave you," the retinue echoed.

"This is all your doing," Mrs Mendelsohn said into Uncle Isaac's face. "You brought the doctor and he, the fool, let these old women in. The work was done before your precious doctor came near the room. You cowardly men are all the same."

"Now be calm, Mrs Mendelsohn!" replied Uncle Isaac patiently. "Are you telling me," he uttered each word with emphasis, "that Doctor McDiarmid, a man of science with degrees from Edinburgh, wasted his time in this room? Do you know where Edinburgh is? Do you know the school of medicine there has a history that—"

He would have continued in his customary way but Mrs Mendelsohn wouldn't hear another word. She said, "I have asked you to take these women outside. If you have no consideration for me at least show some feeling for your wife. She needs rest. Now, please go," she almost shouted the last words.

"Very well," Uncle Isaac said with dignity. But he was a little crestfallen as we left the room, leaving Mrs Mendelsohn alone with Auntie Fanny.

Only a few people remained in the passage as Madame Koch and the old women pattered out of the house, well satisfied with their visit. Uncle Isaac shook hands with them and with all the departing friends. Then he said to me, 'Come, we'll eat something. I'm hungry, would you believe it?"

For the first time I felt sleepy. I had never been up all night before. I almost slept with my head on the kitchen table as Uncle Isaac buttered slices of bread and talked about everything that came into his head. He wondered what his son would be. If only one could see into the future as one could see into the past! He would like to see his son a great scientist or a professor of medicine or a historian.

I closed my eyes but I could still hear Uncle's voice and the crow of the first cock in a distant back-yard and a milk-cart rattling down the lane.

# FATHER'S HORSES

FATHER'S horses were a troublesome lot. Until he acquired Ginger, the tall chestnut gelding, there was something wrong with all of them. But most of them had good looks. Just as it is said that some men are taken in by any pretty woman, so I believe Father couldn't resist a handsome horse, even if warned against it.

There was Prince, whom Father had bought at the horse market. An imposing sight he was in our spring-cart, his velvety black hide, white-stockinged legs, and a white star on his face marked him out from every other hack in the neighbourhood. He had once been a racehorse and it was not Prince's fault that he was now harnessed to a bottle-oh's cart instead of starring on the race track. A trainer and jockey had brought shame on him so that he had been banished for ever from racing. Father could not deny himself the pleasure of telling everyone of his horse's great past and even Mother was obliged to listen to his stories of Prince.

But so long as he had Prince, Father's troubles began every morning as soon as he set out on his bottle round. Whether he was asked to or not the horse would break into a canter and, what was worse, he never wanted to pull up at Father's request. Father shouted at him, cursed him in every language he knew, tugged with all his might on the reins, but Prince could still hear the echoes of pounding hooves and raced on, well past every stopping place.

Then, when at last the horse was prevailed upon to stop, Father had to hurry into back-yards and quickly carry back the empty bottles he had bought. Prince would start suddenly, forcing Father to scramble into the driver's seat and catch hold of the reins just in the nick of time. Regardless of the precious cargo behind Prince cantered flashly and Father, terrified lest we might meet with some mishap, in turn spoke kindly and roared oaths and even raised the whip over the horse's back. But he never really intended to use it. Out of the corner of his eye he would shoot a shamefaced glance at me.

"If I give him the whip he might break into a gallop and we should be finished," he would explain.

Both of us knew that Prince was next to worthless as a bottle-oh's horse, that he was just another one of Father's mistakes.

Then one day things came to a climax.

Prince had been particularly exasperating. He had enjoyed his wild journey and he whinnied happily and shook his mane when he entered our yard. Father jumped off the cart and fastened the wheel. He stood silently staring for a moment at the cart, half empty because of the horse's perversity. He mumbled under his moustache something about a horse sent by the devil to destroy his livelihood and then he strode up to the unsuspecting Prince and struck him hard on the face with his clenched fist. The horse reared back and quivered all over, gazing dumbly at Father.

Father looked round at me, his face twisted sheepishly.

"What did I have to do that for?" he asked in a regretful voice, more to himself than to me. "He's just like a human being, only he's dumb. Why should he know what to do in a bottle-oh's cart? Did I know what to do when I started? He's a gentleman come down in the world. He's not used to earning his living the hard way."

Full of remorse, he tenderly stroked Prince's neck while the horse nuzzled under Father's arm.

"He's got a kind nature," Father said with relief. "He's forgiven me already."

But Father was soon obliged to sell the racehorse. To bottle-ohs and neighbours who inquired after Prince Father vaguely answered that he was too good for a bottle-cart and he hoped that later when he could afford a buggy he would be able to get him back.

After the racehorse there came a sturdy piebald mare. Again beauty beguiled Father. It turned out that she was even worse than Prince. She shied and jibbed and she had an aristocratic taste in food, eating only the finest oaten chaff.

Father was obstinately determined to break the mare to his ways. He refused to look the truth in the face and he maintained that he saw no reason why the mare shouldn't become a good bottle-oh's horse.

"I'll teach her to play up," he would say menacingly. After his experience with Prince he badly needed a victory to restore his self-esteem.

And sometimes for a morning or so it did seem that Father had succeeded. Then he would sigh with relief, stroke his moustache with quiet pride, and nudge me in the ribs.

"See!" He pointed to the broad rump of the jogging mare. "She's as good as gold. It's only a matter of perseverence."

"Well, why does she always shiver when we pass a motor-car?" I asked.

"You and your questions!" he answered irritably. "Do you have to plague me, too?"

But in truth it was not often even Father could pretend that the mare was subdued. Then once the mare shied at a passing motor-car and almost overturned the cart, causing several sacks full of bottles to pitch violently to the ground.

Father and I got down to survey the broken glass strewn dangerously over the road and Father shook his head resignedly, saying, "No one can live a quiet life with a flighty mare. All she wants is food and excitement and she jibs at work. But I'll teach her yet."

But how was he to teach her? He had just about exhausted his patience and store of knowledge when he thought of an acquaintance, a farmer and breeder of horses, who was the right man to teach the mare the hard facts of life.

One morning soon after daybreak we began the long journey to the farm. The sun had just peered over the red rim of the horizon when we left the town shrouded in a white, sugary mist. It was the beginning of spring and the high dome of light-blue sky that stretched to the end of the world was cleanly washed and unflecked by cloud.

We turned off the highway on a narrow, bumpy track between endless rows of tall gum-trees. A heavy aroma of eucalypt, fern, and uncultivated, moist earth arose round us. From high branches magpies carolled to each other as if wondering at the business of the solitary cart below. Our piebald mare unexpectedly pricked up her ears, flung back her head and trotted easily and daintily all the way, with the slight breeze fluttering her long, black mane.

Father gazed gently at her.

"She's different here. The country's good for her nerves," he said.

By midday beyond a bluish haze we could see gleaming sheds and the red iron roof of the farm-house. Far to the side of the house there were several horses grazing with a herd of rusty-brown and white cattle. In a near-by paddock under a solitary tree a chestnut horse stood perfectly still, one rear leg resting on the tip of its hoof.

"There's a sensible animal for you," Father said, peering intently at the chestnut. By then the sun was streaming down from beyond motionless wisps of white cloud.

The farmer's name was Mr Anderson. He and Father sat down on the edge of the veranda and talked about the need for rain, the state of the crops, the low prices received by the man on the land, and the wretched condition of the bottle and bag business. They seemed to enjoy the conversation, for it stretched on and on and neither of them seemed in a hurry to get down to the matter that had brought Father to the farm.

In the warm stillness, broken only by the two voices and the chirping of birds, I sat under a pine-tree near the veranda impatiently waiting for Father and Mr Anderson to finish. Without appetite I ate the sandwiches Mother had prepared and drank milk out of a lemonade bottle, and now and then I idly and viciously threw stones at birds that hopped close to me.

At long last the men rose and walked over to the piebald mare and I hurried after them. With a quick, confident movement of his hands Mr Anderson opened the horse's mouth and peered at her teèth. Then he felt her fetlocks, ran his hand over her belly and concluded his examination by slapping her broad rump.

"A mare's never any good for a cart," he said thoughtfully. "But she'll behave here. My plough horses won't stand any nonsense," he added.

He left us, to fetch the chestnut we had seen sheltering in the shade and when he came back, leading the horse towards us, he spoke to Father.

"If Ginger doesn't suit you can take the mare back. But I bet you'll find the swap to your liking. He's a deep one, is Ginger. Used to be in a baker's cart. Of course he's not as young as the mare, but he's got more up top," he concluded, pointing to his own head.

Father said nothing and eyed the chestnut suspiciously. The horse was not much to look at and I imitated Father's appraising stare. After the mare it did seem a bit of a comedown to think of riding behind such an ungainly brute.

The mare was quickly unharnessed and Ginger backed into the shafts. He seemed quite content with his new lot, for he made no protest and responded promptly to Father's orders. But Father wouldn't let me on the cart with him until he had properly tested the chestnut. He drove him round the yard, stopped and started a number of times, backed, got off the cart and on again, while Mr Anderson created a frightful din by banging on a kerosene tin and shouting to show off the horse's steady nerves. Ginger passed all tests with honour and he was ours.

Despite the satisfactory deal, Father's heart was heavy all the way back to the town at parting with so pretty a horse as the piebald mare. He said he hoped Mr Anderson wouldn't use the whip on her. He was sure she had looked back reproachfully at him when he left the farm. No doubt if Ginger had been a good-looking horse Father would have been less worried about the fate of the mare.

Pointing his whip at the chestnut, he said, "Look at the ugly beast! His tail sweeps up the dust, his belly sags, his

rump swings like a pendulum. And look at those tufts of
hair around his hooves." And he added disgustedly, "What
a nag!"

But Father was soon obliged to admit grudgingly that as
a worker Ginger was far superior to any other horse he had
had. Ginger was good-tempered and never endangered the
bottles. But he had a strong will, and he would not be hurried; no amount of shouting or shaking of the reins or
cracking of the whip could alter his pace. Whether the cart
was loaded with bagged bottles or quite empty made no
difference; Ginger kept the same easy pace. Secretly I felt
superior to Father, who seemed unable to exercise any
control over the horse. I fancied that if only I had the
opportunity I would make the horse do my bidding.

There were other ways, too, in which Father was obliged
to bow to Ginger's will. Every lunch-time he was obliged
to wait, fretting and fuming, until Ginger had devoured his
last scrap of chaff. On the few occasions when Father had
tried to take a partly filled nosebag away from him he had
bared his teeth and snapped at him. So, as Ginger was a
slow eater, Father, for the first time in his life, had to take
his time over his own food.

But more than anything else Ginger angered Father with
his habit of turning into streets that he had once worked
in. In these streets he would stop at every second house
just as he had when he was in the baker's cart and Father
was helpless to do anything about it. If the street turned
out to be full of bottles Father would excuse himself by
saying that it didn't matter where he bought bottles any
way. But if the houses were bare of bottles he would hurl
curses at Ginger's head, saying, "I've got a boss sitting on

top of my head. He tells me where to buy bottles. A plague on him."

Whenever Father was especially irritated with Ginger and chagrined by his ineffectual struggles to bend the horse to his will he thought regretfully of Prince and the mare. He would sing their praises as if nothing had happened to mar his delight in their beauty. Then he would profess to see no virtue in Ginger.

"He's as ugly as sin, and pot-bellied into the bargain," he said. "He's old and as cunning as a fox. Why did he have to fall into my hands?"

Father's battle with Ginger became a subject of conversation and humour amongst the Jewish bottle-ohs and dealers that we met on our rounds and at the bottle-yards.

We met a group of them one lunch-time at a horse trough on the outskirts of the town. They were sitting by the side of the road, eating their sandwiches whilst their horses ate and rested.

After Ginger had drunk from the trough Father led him to a tree where he could eat his chaff in the shade. Then we sat down on the ground close to the others to eat our hard-boiled eggs and bread and butter.

One of the dealers, who bought rabbit skins and hides, pointed to Ginger and said in a grave voice, "I can see your nag's a real bargain. I'm the Prince of Wales if he's a day under twelve years. You should put him in the Show. He'd take a prize."

Another bottle-oh spoke up in a slow, astonished voice. "You know, forgive me for saying this, you're getting to look like your horse. That comes of letting him lead you by the nose. It's the same when you let a wife lead you by the nose, you lose your own features and begin to look like her."

Involuntarily I looked round at the horse and then at Father. Surely it was absurd, yet there did seem to be some resemblance between the two; it must have been Father's red moustache and the gingery stubble on his face.

I wanted to join in the laughter but Father's face deterred me. I knew he was not to be lightly laughed at and from his eyes I guessed he was just about to overflow.

Another bottle-oh, encouraged by the laughter, roared, "Your nag sweats like a fat old pig."

Father rose to his feet. Livid with rage, he shouted into the man's face, "If I harnessed you in the cart and stuck a straw in your rear and shouted, 'Gid up, my good brother!' you would surely look like a pig even more than Ginger."

There was a hush. Just then Ginger gave an exhibition of bad manners.

"That's what he thinks of your talk," Father jeered.

Taken aback by Father's anger the bottle-ohs and dealers began to placate him.

"We didn't mean anything," one said.

"If the horse suits you, he suits us," another said.

But they stayed round no longer and as they drove away they shouted farewells.

"Have a good day."

"Go with good health."

For all this Father still smarted from their remarks. He muttered, "What have they got against my horse? An honest worker who gives no one any trouble. And they laugh at him and tear him to pieces! Some people try to belittle anyone they think will stand for it. They try to feel their strength even at the expense of a horse. Upon my word, it's a nasty world."

Father's affection for Ginger dated from this encounter. He no longer spoke harshly of him nor would he allow any-one else to do so. He even began to overlook his appearance, saying that it was after all character that mattered.

How fond Father had become of Ginger I was soon to learn to my own cost.

He had pulled up outside the only house in a street more like a bush track, some distance from a tram terminus. Father told me to stay on the cart and after fastening the wheel he disappeared into the house.

For a short time I gazed round at the quiet surroundings. In the distance I could hear the clanging of trams and the tapping of a hammer in a partly-built house in a far-off pad-dock. There was not a voice to be heard nor a dog to be seen. In the mid-afternoon summer stillness the birds seemed to have gone to sleep.

I soon began to fret with impatience. It seemed as if hours had passed since I had last seen Father. I called to Ginger, who was cropping grass at his hooves and lazily switching his tail. He made no response and continued to chew, his head bent to the ground. Bored at having nothing to do and irritated with the horse who refused to acknow-ledge my commands, I grasped the reins and tugged on them. I pulled with all my strength until Ginger raised his head ever so slightly and then he shook it impatiently and returned to his eating.

Slowly a savage idea began to form in my mind. Even if Father was helpless before Ginger and had succumbed to his ways I would show him that I was made of different stuff. All my dislike for the horse welled up in me as I held the reins with one hand and picked up the whip with the other and waved it in the air.

Then I let the whip fall lightly on Ginger's back. He reared his head suddenly and I shouted, "Gid up!" But he didn't budge and this time I struck at him harder. He snorted and stamped his hooves and I lashed at him again and again.

Flecks of saliva appeared on his mouth as he champed the bit, and he suddenly pulled the cart forward a few feet. But the chain fastened round the wheel brought him to a sudden stop.

Delighted with my success I shouted, "Gid up!" again and raised the whip, but at that moment Father appeared at the gate of the house, carrying a bag of bottles over his shoulder. I dropped the whip to the floor and smiled at Father as though nothing had happened. He ignored my smile, pretending that he hadn't seen me, lowered the bottles to the ground and walked over to the horse. Gently he stroked Ginger's face and mumbled, "What's he been doing to you, eh?"

As though satisfied with the horse's reply he walked with affected calm to the cart and got in beside me. Without looking in my direction he said quietly, "So that's what you do when my back it turned? You torment animals, eh? I suppose there isn't an animal safe from your paws unless it can bite."

When he finished talking he suddenly gripped me strongly with one arm and turned me over his knee.

I can't remember how many times his heavy hand fell on my backside but I can still recall his hot breath on my neck and his words in my ears.

"You can pretend the horse is hitting you back, you cruel scamp. You'll remember next time when your hand itches to torment somebody. This'll teach you to respect horses that work for their living, you rascal."

The punishment over, Father got off the cart to fetch the bottles he had left on the ground. He walked with slow, exaggeratedly dignified steps, but he glanced round furtively to see if anybody was in sight. There was no one.

# NEIGHBOURS

OUR next-door neighbours arrived in the morning. It was still cold, for the sun had not yet risen over the roofs.

The street re-echoed with the stamping of horses' hooves and the voices of neighbours who had just come out from breakfast. Our street was a narrow, cobbled one—a cul-de-sac of nondescript houses with tiny verandas and wooden fences right on the footpath.

The new-comers' wagon was piled higgledy-piggledy with stretchers, chairs, wooden boxes, pots and pans. There were ten in the family.

The older ones helped their father to carry the furniture into the house while their mother saw to the younger ones. She ushered them to the veranda and fed them with biscuits and apples.

We children clustered round the wagon, getting under the feet of the workers and gingerly patting the stamping, steaming horses. We chattered and laughed and furtively peered into the dark, musty recesses of the open door of the empty house. It was like all the others in the street and had a low, slanting, galvanized-iron roof, a rusty, crooked chimney, and blistered, brown wooden walls.

As the commotion grew one of the boys who had been helping his father abruptly left his work. With his hands on his hips, he said challengingly to the boys around, "I'll race you to end of the street."

We stared at him with curious eyes. He was about eleven years of age and came somewhere in the middle of the family. His straight black hair and his narrow slits of eyes immediately earned him the name of "Chinaman". He was short and slender, but he gazed at us as boldly as a lion Like his brothers and sisters he was poorly dressed in some blue, cheap stuff and his sandshoes were grimy and thread-bare.

"Tell us your name and we'll race you," said Joseph, eye-ing the new-comer with a sceptical look. Joseph was the tallest and strongest boy in our group and our acknowledged leader.

"Benny Smutkevitch," came the instant reply.

We lined up in the middle of the road, completely absorbed in our new interest. Forgotten were the horses, the wagon, and Benny's family. And the adults standing behind the fences and in the street scarcely gave us a glance, so accustomed were they to our noisy play.

Benny made us look very foolish. He shot off the mark and flew to the end of the street, leaving the rest of us behind running clumsily like broken-winded old horses.

"Give in?" he said cheekily, fixing a triumphant gaze on us.

"No, I won't give in," said Joseph, still panting from his strenuous efforts to catch Benny.

"You won't?" said Benny. "Well, I'll race you back hopping."

"Hoppo bumpo first," said Joseph with a sly look. Con-fident of his strength, he was anxious to beat Benny in a bumping contest on one leg.

"Make a ring," shouted several voices.

Benny and Joseph hopped towards each other with a business-like air. Arms folded, each endeavoured to bump the other to the ground. Excitedly we closed in on the com-batants. Despite our dwindling confidence in Joseph we shouted words of encouragement to him. He looked much the stronger of the two.

Benny hopped with an incredibly long step like a kangaroo and all Joseph's efforts to reach him were in vain. He soon tired of missing Benny and he stopped in the centre of the ring, biting his lips with vexation.

One boy shouted to him, "Don't rush! Take your time."

"Your legs are made of wood and your bottom is too large," another voice said in disgust.

Joseph turned to his detractor with a threatening air and in that moment he was bumped off his feet by Benny, who came at him with great speed.

"Foul!" shouted several boys.

Our leader sprawled on the cobbled ground. We made one more attempt to best Benny before admitting his superiority. The same boys who had shouted, "Foul!" now cried, "All together, at him!"

The howl of voices brought Benny's elder brothers to the scene. They stood on the edge of the compressed ring, frowning bad-temperedly. But Benny was in no need of their assistance, for he was scattering us to the ground like a chaff-cutter. With deadly purpose he had increased his tempo, and shouting insults he leapt first at one and then at another.

At the height of the mêlée a little girl more curious than the others strayed into the moving, swaying ring. She was promptly knocked over and lay on the ground whimpering and sobbing. Her mother, who had been watching us from a distance, came running distractedly towards us.

"Stop this hooliganism!" Mrs Katz shrieked. "You young hooligans! You will bring eternal shame on your parents!" she went on as she stooped to help her daughter to her feet.

She cast angry looks at us, staring fixedly first at one and then another as if attempting to discover who had knocked her daughter over.

Her shrill agitated voice brought the encounter to an end; only Benny was still dancing round, his black, glossy hair tossed over his forehead, his fists clenched in readiness.

"Who did it?" she inquired of her daughter loudly. We shuffled backwards, trying to efface ourselves. None of us was eager to brave Mrs Katz.

She was a short, big-bosomed woman with a fat and rosy face. Her life seemed to consist of keeping an eternal eye on her only child. She had already quarrelled with all the other women in the street over the misdemeanours of their boys and girls and she was for ever upbraiding us.

"It was him," the little girl tearfully pointed to Benny.

Mrs Katz turned angrily to face Benny.

"Look," she said in her shrill voice, indicating with her hand a bruise on the girl's leg and dust marks on her white dress. "Look what you have done to her."

I sighed with relief, and so did the other boys, that Benny was blamed and not us. Benny reluctantly moved towards the wagon, pushed forward by Mrs Katz.

Her shouts had meanwhile drawn the attention of some of the other women who began to call their children inside. As if to pour salt into his wound, Joseph's mother cried to him, "Come inside at once!"

Thoroughly shamefaced, his eyes averted from us, our former leader ran quickly at his mother's call. Cruel voices shouted after him, "Sissy! Cry-baby!"

From then on we deserted Joseph and our new allegiance was to Benny. We watched him admiringly from afar. His short, lithe body stood beside his father at the back of the wagon in front of the low wooden house. He seemed full of a reckless vitality.

"You should control your boy," Mrs Katz waved an aggressive finger. "He's not a boy, he's a wild animal. That's what he is, a wild animal," she stammered on a grating top note into Mr Smutkevitch's face.

His short-sighted, red-rimmed grey eyes darted round piercingly from Mrs Katz and her daughter to Benny.

Mr Smutkevitch was a middle-sized, thick-set man with red hair. His huge red beard covered all his face except the eyes and nose, and it was stained with black snuff marks round his hairy nostrils. There was only a tight slit to mark his mouth.

He swayed impatiently on his slightly bowed legs as Mrs Katz continued her recital. All the time his face was swelling with anger like a turkey-cock. At last he raised a gnarled, freckled hand.

"Enough," he said gruffly.

Without making another sound he suddenly turned to Benny and struck him quickly and dexterously once, twice, on both cheeks. Then, casting an unfriendly glance at Mrs Katz, he climbed back on the wagon, beckoned to his two elder sons, and began handing down pieces of furniture. Not a word did he speak.

All this happened so quickly that Mrs Katz remained standing open-mouthed, her brows knitted in perplexity. This was not what she had expected and it seemed to me that she was assailed by a sudden pity for Benny.

"Mr Smutkevitch," she began, looking up at the unresponsive face. "Mr Smutkevitch—" and then she stopped and cleared her throat.

Meantime, Benny's mother, who had witnessed the scene from the veranda, shuffled with a sideways gait into the street and looked round at the strange faces. With motherly concern she made for Benny. She whispered to him as she stroked his head.

Mrs Smutkevitch was like her boy; the same long slits of black eyes, thick spreading line of brows and olive skin. Her smoothly combed, gleaming black hair, gathered in a heavy knot at the back, showed her anxious, unhappy face.

"What have you got against my child?" she asked, suddenly turning to Mrs Katz. "Why did you have to interfere with the children?" she went on in a flat, whimpering voice.

"Don't get upset," said Mrs Katz. "Let's talk it over reasonably."

"Grown-ups should keep out of children's affairs. You interfered cruelly," Mrs Smutkevitch said, looking down at the ground.

"Please listen to me for a moment," Mrs Katz began. But Mrs Smutkevitch interrupted her, not permitting her to finish a sentence.

Then Mr Smutkevitch, standing on the tailboard of the wagon and without glancing at the two women, shouted as if into the air, "Stop that old wives' quarrel!"

His gruff, impatient voice resounded down the street. There was silence. Fixing his short-sighted stare on his wife, he shouted again, "Take the boy inside! I don't want to hear another word."

The new family was on the lips of everybody in the street. My mother thought very badly of Mr Smutkevitch. The way he had spoken to his wife was insufferable! Why, he had shouted at her like a sergeant-major! Others said they could see that Benny was no precious toy. They would have to watch him with cats' eyes.

We boys, however, regarded Benny as our new leader and hero. Each of us separately sought his special favour. We gave him marbles, picture-books, penny dreadfuls, Buffalo Bills, cigarette-cards, pocket-knives, and other odds and ends. He quickly understood that we were like putty in his hands and preferred none of us as his best friend. So he soon acquired a prodigious fortune out of our generosity, though his father never gave him any pocket-money and never bought him presents. But Benny soon tired of these petty dealings. He was full of plans for adventures in which we figured as his followers.

Thus began a new chapter in our lives.

Unbeknown to our parents we sneaked away from the street one summer day. My mother had always forbidden me to go beyond the street, but what could I do when Benny asked me to go with him and the others in a jaunt to the river that flowed through the city? His confident face, his narrow slits of mocking eyes, and his careless hands on hips shamed me into violating Mother's orders.

Another time Benny took us to a circus and we stood outside the tent and listened to the bandsmen in blue and gold uniforms play "Pack up Your Troubles" and "It's a Long Way to Tipperary". We caught a glimpse of the elephants and the monkeys, and Benny, who had read tales of hunters and explorers, airily told us that one day he would leave for a place far away to hunt animals as remarkable as the bunyip. We believed him and marvelled at his nonchalant courage.

Then another time, not far from our street we met a group of boys playing in a vacant paddock. Benny sat down on the uncut grass and we slavishly followed suit. Insolently he began to jeer and laugh at the playing boys. They stopped their game and stared at us. Then they cried, "Ikey Mo!" and wagged their outstretched palms under their chins. Before we could rise to our feet they began to throw clods of earth and stones at us. Benny was ready for them. Using a kerosene tin as a shield he shied empty jam tins at our enemies. He was playing at war but his army was badly trained and quite unused to such earnest encounters. We turned tail and ran and our backs bore the marks of our defeat.

Our secret life was not known to our parents, but on this occasion the tell-tale marks of dust and grime on my clothes had given me away. My disreputable appearance loomed tragically in Mother's eyes and she spoke scathingly of this new land where children defied their parents and roamed the streets like wild dogs.

But my mother, like the other women in the street, found excuses for her own child. It was all Benny's doing. Benny was to blame for everything. And so the women began to think that perhaps they should approach Mr Smutkevitch and appeal to him to restrain his son for the good of the street. Although Mr Smutkevitch rarely spoke to anyone and his gruff, frightening manner had not been forgotten, the women began to think better of him, and even Mother said that perhaps he was deserving of some sympathy on account of his wayward and vagrant son.

Two women were deputed to talk to Mr Smutkevitch and they waited for him at the gate of his house. As soon as the wagon approached Mr Smutkevitch pulled tightly on the reins, stood up in the driver's seat, and shouted above the heads of the women to his little girls playing on the veranda, "Tell your mother to have my tea on the table! I'm in a hurry."

Without turning his eyes in the direction of the women or bidding them a good day, he jumped off the wagon with sure-footed agility and ran into the house. The two women shuffled their feet and coughed and said nothing. They became ashamed of their previous good words about Mr Smutkevitch and hurried back to their homes, loudly cursing the family that had brought such unpleasantness to the street. Too proud to discuss things with women, they said, 'A plague on him and that boy of his! Like father, like son!"

We were forbidden to play with Benny or to call at his home. I ignored Mother's orders and one morning just before breakfast I peered through the kitchen door of the Smutkevitch house. I hoped to see Benny and to arrange to walk to school with him.

I was met by the sight of father and sons, their hats on their heads, standing facing the eastern wall of the room, reciting morning prayers. Mr Smutkevitch and the two older boys wore phylacteries and read from their prayer books, but Benny and the younger ones were not yet old enough to wear the tiny sacred leather cases containing the holy parchment. They mumbled the words, their eyes moving idly towards the door.

Mr Smutkevitch's phylacteries were carefully adjusted to his head and arm and the thong was neatly tied on the arm, palm, and finger. He prayed slowly, enunciating each holy word in a rapture of loving tenderness. His stern face was wrinkled by a secretive smile, something between him and God.

But the phylacteries seemed a burden on the two older boys. They continually fingered the leather-covered cases and gabbled the prayers with sullen expressions on their faces. With sleepy eyes they shot malevolent glances at Benny, and I guessed they were filled with envy of him, who would soon run freely into the street while they would have to go to their daily work, the elder to help his father on the bottle-cart, the other' to a tailor's shop.

As soon as the prayers were over Mr Smutkevitch lovingly bound up his phylacteries and replaced them in their embroidered velvet bag. His face again became angry and stern and I sidled out into the yard.

Suddenly Mr Smutkevitch's voice filled the small kitchen and I listened intently.

"You heretic!" I heard him shout at Benny. "Your father's ways don't suit you? Ah? You think your ways are better? If I ever catch you staying away from the scripture lessons I will break every bone in your body!"

Then Mrs Smutkevitch's flat, pleading voice floated out to me.

"I will see he goes to his lessons. Benny will be a good boy, won't you, Benny? You will do what your father tells you?"

But the next sabbath Benny sidled out of the synagogue under the very nose of his father. I saw Mr Smutkevitch's face darken and his body swayed more vigorously as if seeking solace in his prayers. Without taking his eyes from the prayer book in front of him, he laid one hand gently on his eldest son's arm to deter him from following Benny into the street. It was as if he had decided that for the moment it was better to let one carry the sins of the family.

We knew that Benny had hurried out to meet his new friend, Martin Gallagher, and his departure threw us into a state of agitated curiosity so that we were deaf to the ardent praying round us. A bolder one amongst us stole towards the door. Then we all rose from our pews and guiltily tiptoed right out of the darkened, murmuring synagogue into the sunlit street outside.

On the next corner Martin and Benny were whispering together in some strange gibberish. They had manufactured their own language, and we offered them new marbles and tops to disclose the secrets of the fascinating code to us, but without any success. They regarded themselves as something apart from us.

Martin and Benny were a strange contrast; Martin was as fair as Benny was dark and he was at least a head taller. He was dressed in a thin, butcher-blue suit and he was barefooted. His great boast was that he could walk on broken glass without cutting his feet. They were leathery and always caked with brown dust. Martin came from a mysterious world. His father was at the war and he never mentioned his mother or sisters or brothers, if indeed he had any.

"Coming with us?" Martin said with a mischievous wink at Benny. They looked at each other knowingly.

We were flattered by the invitation, for Martin as a rule never spoke to us without screwing up his face and jabbering in his own mysterious language.

"Cross your hearts," he commanded us.

And we had to swear not to tell our parents.

I crossed my heart fearfully, with one reluctant finger, feeling all the world like a traitor and an apostate and imagining that the beadle was standing on the steps of the synagogue and watching my heretical motions.

Martin and Benny led us through streets and lanes to a park crowded with men and women. They were standing round a man in a brown cloth cap who spoke from a pulpit-like wooden platform in the shade of an elm-tree. His face red with exertion, he said in a loud voice that the war was for the master class. His words roused shouts of disapproval and there was a movement of people towards the speaker. The excitement infected every one of us and our hesitation and fears left us.

Following Martin and Benny we wove through the crowd, stepping on feet and being jostled and pushed in the back. As we came closer to the platform the speaker's words resounded in our ears. He was denouncing the conscription of men for the army, and this was something that had begun to stir our street.

Angry voices again rose from the crowd and several men in uniform pushed their way towards the platform. Other men formed a ring round the speaker and blows were struck as the soldiers tried to push the platform over.

Suddenly a woman screamed. The wooden platform lay on the ground and the crowd behind merged with the milling soldiers and men gathered round the hapless speaker. A squad of policemen appeared from nowhere and mingled with the crowd. Wildly excited, we boys ran to the outskirts of the moving, swaying mass of people and shouted words that had no meaning.

Very soon the police drew their batons and the dull, empty thud of wood on flesh resounded sickeningly. We stopped in our wild caperings and gazed open-mouthed.

Barely able to restrain a sob of fear when a policeman with baton in hand brushed past me, I fled from the park.

Some of my companions soon caught up with me. We glanced back for a moment and behind the trees at the end of the park rose the tall buildings of the city. We could hear the sharp clatter of the cable trams and we walked on in bleak silence, towards our homes. Neither Martin nor Benny was with us.

The news of our behaviour in the synagogue reached home before we did. Mr Applebaum, the beadle, had shuffled along from house to house apologetically blowing his nose as he complained of us. And Mrs Katz stood in front of the gate of her home and shook her head at us as we hurried past and shouted, "You young scoundrels! You will drive your mothers to their graves!"

Mother was not at all surprised at Mr Applebaum's information. She had a premonition, she said, that her son would become like Martin if we stayed in this country. In a few years' time Benny and her own son would be strangers to their parents.

Father made light of the whole affair and tried to placate Mother.

"Don't take it so much to heart," he said. "There are many attractions outside a synagogue for a boy of his age. Why, even I ran away myself when I was a boy."

And then he plunged into a story of his childhood, boastfully relating how he had tormented his old Rabbi in his town in Russia. I laughed more than was necessary and he suddenly broke off his story and fixed me with an angry glare. My laugh had unexpectedly offended him and he went pale in the face.

"I'll give you something you'll never forget if you cause your mother any more anguish," he said. "Now, pick up your Hebrew book and go into your room and don't let me hear a whisper out of you. Now go." His voice brooked no contradiction. You can't rely on Father, I thought, as I hurried out of the room.

I was not the only boy who was punished. Others suffered more severely, and Benny was thrashed by his father and then locked up in the shed with the horses and bottles.

Mr Smutkevitch was still in a savage temper at Mr Frumkin's bottle-yard the following Friday. He was arguing heatedly with Mr Frumkin as we drove into the yard.

It was just past noon. The sky overhead was blue and bright and there was a pleasant late spring heat in the air. There were many men in the big yard and they were moving about with great determination. They carried sacks into open sheds and stacked bottles into crates.

Suddenly they looked up from their work and turned towards the two quarrelling men. Father jumped off the cart, leaving me holding the reins, and moved with the others over to Mr Smutkevitch and Mr Frumkin.

Mr Frumkin had grown stouter. He still wore the same dust-covered trousers but the top buttons were undone and his open waistcoat was held together by a massive gold chain. From under his new black borsalino hat he squinted sideways at Mr Smutkevitch, who was angrily demanding a better price for a neat stack of glossy new chaff-bags lying at his feet.

"I won't give you that price," said Mr Frumkin, jingling a pocket full of coins with his thick, sausage-like fingers.

"How am I to feed my family?" asked Mr Smutkevitch with a momentary expression of despair on his red-bearded face. "I work like a horse but I'm not fed like one," he added bitterly.

He spoke so feelingly that Mr Frumkin smiled secretly to himself as though pleased and flattered that the unbending and taciturn Mr Smutkevitch was thus forced to appeal to him.

"Well, I'll lend you some money," said Mr Frumkin expansively. "I won't see you starve."

Mr Smutkevitch's short, stout neck went red with anger and for a moment I was afraid he would have a fit. Clenching his fists, the muscles of his cheeks quivering, he spoke with great difficulty as if suppressing a torrent of frightful words.

"You grind us into the earth and then you offer to buy us a coffin."

"Are you doing me a favour by turning my offer down?" Mr Frumkin turned to the others with a humorous gesture of the hands. "If you are so independent," he continued slowly, "you can work the whole of Friday and even Saturday. I keep my yard open for those who are not Rabbis."

"How dare you talk to me like that, you apostate!" Mr Smutkevitch cried to Mr Frumkin in a hoarse, panting voice. "You wicked apostate!"

With quick, impulsive movements Mr Smutkevitch tossed the bags on his wagon and as he placed one foot on the step he glanced back at Mr Frumkin. Turning his head from side to side he made as if to spit on the ground and then, swinging the reins over his horses' heads, he drove out of the yard.

I saw Mr Smutkevitch again near the door of the synagogue on the sabbath. I was surprised to see him outside, for the service was not yet finished. He was talking to Mr Applebaum. The beadle had one leg inside the synagogue and one outside and he was chewing at his nails, as was his habit, and looking at the ground. Mr Applebaum was tall and lean and he had a pale, melancholy face. He now seemed more melancholy than ever.

With an impatient shrug of his shoulders Mr Smutkevitch abruptly turned his back on the beadle and advanced towards me.

"Have you seen my Ben?" He stared at me with a mournful, vexed expression in his short-sighted, red-rimmed eyes.

I made no reply, merely shaking my head nervously.

"I will find him," he said, scowling at me.

Instead of going on into the synagogue I followed Mr Smutkevitch. He stopped a passing boy, who was carrying in his hand a velvet bag containing a prayer book and shawl, and appeared to be making inquiries.

I knew where Benny was to be found. He had gone to a church hall in the street behind the synagogue. There was to be a fair in the afternoon and Martin had asked us all to go with him and watch the preparations.

Even now, when I was resolved to warn Benny that his father was looking for him, I hesitated to go near a church. It was a warm, windy December morning and a fine grit assailed my face and hands as I walked with a heavy heart towards the hall. Pieces of paper flew past me. Behind me the swiftly-moving white clouds seemed peppered with a grey dust.

I stopped outside the wooden hall. Benny and Martin and several other boys were standing in the doorway. From within came the sound of merry voices and the noise of feet sliding on the polished floor.

I looked up at the plain wooden cross above the door. My heart fluttered with terror as I sidled closer to Benny.

I whispered to him about his father and pleaded with him to hasten away with me. Although I knew that stalls and lucky-dip bins were being placed in position for the afternoon fair, I was terrified of looking inside. I trembled at the thought of standing under the cross on the sabbath.

Benny seemed no more comfortable than I was, but he was unable to make up his mind to leave. In the meantime the other boys had walked into the hall, leaving him and me standing at the door.

Minutes seemed to pass. I stared at the street and in the distance I could already see Mr Smutkevitch walking towards us. He peered intently. Then he caught sight of Benny. Their eyes met and Mr Smutkevitch stopped at a distance, but neither spoke.

At that moment Martin and several other boys came out of the hall, excitedly calling to us, "Come in."

They stopped and their gaze followed ours.

Mr Smutkevitch beckoned Benny with one broad, heavy finger. Suddenly Martin and his friends began to mimic Mr Smutkevitch with their fingers. They shouted at him in their strange gibberish. He looked bewildered and grinned foolishly, his red beard parting for a moment.

Out of the corner of my eye I saw Benny wince. He tried to efface himself behind the backs of the boys. His eyes darted nervously to and fro in their narrow slits. His face quivered and beads of sweat came out on his forehead.

The boys quickly tired of their mimicry and ran shouting back into the hall, leaving Benny and me to face Mr Smutkevitch.

There was a stubborn, angry look on Mr Smutkevitch's face as he cast a last glance at us. He turned away slowly, his shoulders momentarily hunched as if he had suddenly become an old man.

As his broad back and bowed legs became smaller in the distance Benny ran into the street as if to follow his father. Then he stopped. There was a look of anxiety in his dark, nimble eyes and we did not speak to one another as we walked on, but neither of us knew that there could be no reconciliation with the ways of our fathers.

# BLACK GIRL

LILY SAMUELS lived with her family in a condemned two-story building which had once been a shop and a residence. They lived in this derelict place because they were unable to find accommodation in any other part of the city and because they were aborigines. Our landlord, who owned a good many houses in the street, readily let the disused building to the aboriginal family for a small rental.

It was the only tall building in the neighbourhood; the rest were low, shrunken, and wedged together. From the broken windows of the second story the tenants could look into the back-yards of all the houses, or upwards along the roof-tops to the broad, tree-lined avenue and the park on the rise beyond. The lofty walls of their bare rooms were gashed and punctured with long, twisting cracks and holes, and a pale green flake from the blistered plaster on the ceiling fell constantly on the floor.

The Samuels had brought very little furniture with them. There were several black iron beds, three rickety wooden chairs, the legs tied with wire, and boxes of all shapes and sizes. These boxes served as chairs, tables, and toys for the children who slept upstairs on bags and tattered mattresses on the worn, loose floor-boards.

There was no proper kitchen or dining-room and the family ate in the room that had once been a store-room at the back of the old shop. On the stained and blotched plaster above the only tap in the house, hung brightly coloured butchers' and bakers' calendars and at the side a number of shelves of plain deal had been screwed into the wall. On these shelves stood open tins of sweetened milk, treacle and jam, a bag of flour, and loaves of bread.

Disorder reigned at meal times when the children sat down on the floor or on boxes to chew bread thickly smeared with treacle or jam. There were so many children that it was likely they were not all brothers and sisters, but all answered to the name of Samuels. They were fed by Lily, who was the eldest girl and took care of them most of the time, since Mr Samuels and his wife were often away.

Laughter and screams could be heard at every meal time, right down the whole length of the street. And this immoderate merriment caused unfriendly comment from some of the people in the neighbourhood. It was as though they saw something mocking and menacing in the carefree gaiety of the black children.

Mr Johnson was especially vociferous in his condemnation of the family. No girl as young as Lily should be left in charge of such a large, wild brood, and besides he knew what black girls of fifteen or so were like. They were frivolous and worse. They could not be trusted.

Mr Johnson was a lean, tall, sallow-faced man, nearly always clad in a grey flannel, and his braces often trailed at his slippered feet. He worked only on Fridays and Saturdays at a stall on the markets so that for the rest of the week he was able to keep a sharp eye on everyone.

He had some reason for his watchfulness. In his back-yard he kept pigeons and his aviary was constantly under our eyes. In addition every spare inch of his tiny yard was filled with boxes in which grew flowers and vegetables. Even the roofs of the shed and laundry were covered with a maze of greenery.

He was very proud of his garden, but his pleasure was permanently blighted by the fear that sooner or later all his loving handiwork would be destroyed. His padlocked gate with the sign, "Beware of the Dog," and the large, shiny, brass knocker on the door glared warningly at us.

We watched him promenade slowly up and down in front of the houses, his thin nostrils twitching disdainfully as if there was a bad smell under his nose all the time. Stolidly he kept his eyes averted from some Jewish women standing in front of their houses. He had more than once exchanged hot words with them.

He stopped for a moment before the open door of the Samuels house. From the darkness within a pungent odour escaped—the odour of musty dampness, human bodies crowded together, dirty linen, and stale food that might have been left and forgotten. Mr Johnson pressed his lips tightly together, sniffed, and hurried back to his home, muttering all the while.

He carefully unlocked the padlock, opened the iron-spiked gate a little, sidled in and locked the gate again. Clenching the top of a spike with one fist, he stood behind the gate and called to his boy, Harry, who was playing with us.

"If you ever bring any of those abo kids around here," he said curtly, "I'll wring your blooming neck, so help me." And then, addressing us all, he added, "If you take my tip you'll all stay away from that Lily and the rest of them."

His vehement advice fell on stony ears. Even Harry, who took after his father inasmuch as he always called us dirty Jew boys when we quarrelled, came with us when we made down the footpath towards the two-story house.

We crowded round the open door and listened to the childish voices that floated out to us. Without knocking or announcing ourselves, we rowdily trooped through the dim rooms, staring curiously into every corner until we reached the sunlit back-yard. I was relieved that neither Mr nor Mrs Samuels was at home.

We were met by the sight of Lily nursing an infant in her arms in the middle of a ring of boys and girls holding hands and moving slowly and rhythmically in time to their own singing. Only Charlie Samuels played on his own. He squatted on his heels against the high wooden fence and drew designs in the sand with his fingers. He looked up lazily and rose slowly to his feet. A stocky, surly little figure, he cast a distrustful glance at us.

Lily seemed at a loss for something to say to us. For a moment she did not know how to treat her uninvited guests. She gazed uneasily from beneath unruly, thick black eyebrows. Her dark, soft eyes moved nervously to and fro in their oval slits.

"Join hands," she said suddenly. "We'll play oranges and lemons."

We looked at each other with sheepish grins and made no move towards the group of children.

"Come and join hands with Florrie," Lily said, smiling at me and beckoning to me with one finger. A breeze slightly fluttered her rose-coloured skirt and played with her black, coppery-tinted hair. Her pink blouse tucked into her skirt tightly embraced her breasts and slender shoulders.

Bashfully I did as she asked me. But my companions turned their backs on me and wandered along the fence, idly examining the saplings, kerosene tins, and broken bits of furniture that littered the yard. Charlie shuffled towards them.

I linked hands with Florrie and Lily began to sing in a thin, high-pitched tremolo and the others joined in as they moved under our swinging arms.

We had almost reached the words "head off" and we were about to claim our first captive when a commotion from the end of the yard brought our game to a sudden end. Lily ran over to the boys near the fence.

"Give it back to me!" Harry Johnson shouted, tugging at Charlie's sleeve. "I want my top. He took it off me," he added indignantly to Lily.

"Give it back to him, Charlie," Lily said quietly.

Suddenly Charlie raised a fist with the top tightly enclosed and struck Harry on the nose with great force. Then with the other fist he struck him twice on the cheek. Whimpering, Harry retreated with the other boys who gave ground as Charlie advanced, both fists up.

Her protruding lip trembling, Lily caught hold of Charlie's shirt with her free hand and pulled him towards her.

"You shouldn't have done that. You shouldn't have hit him," she admonished him.

Held firmly, Charlie fixed wild eyes on Harry's face and his pallid, broad palms with the pink fingernails fluttered excitedly. Harry was tenderly stroking his face and rubbing his nose. As soon as he saw a streak of blood on the back of his hand his eyes filled with tears and he began to sob with fear. Without taking the top now being offered to him by one of Lily's sisters who had picked it up from the ground, he ran crying through the house into the street.

The other boys were already half-way through the house

when I hurried after them, though I should have liked to stay with Lily. She followed behind, blocking from sight her sisters and brothers, and for the first time for many a day she closed the front door.

At the end of the street Mr Johnson was talking angrily to a group of neighbours. Thoroughly nettled by this latest incident, he stormed against the aboriginal family.

"I told them to keep away from those stinking, thieving abos. But they didn't do what I told them. Abos shouldn't be allowed to live among white people."

That evening I was again in the street. On both sides men and women sat on chairs under their tiny verandas. The air was still and hot. Heavy sombre clouds floated sluggishly across the pale high sky. The two feeble street lamps had not yet been lit. In the distance we could just make out Mr Samuels and his wife.

Their progress down the street was followed by curious eyes. After Mr Johnson's strong words, we waited expectantly for God knows what to happen. But no one spoke, and Mr Johnson remained mute behind his padlocked gate. Only Mr Samuels shot a sullen glance at someone who had stared a moment too long at him. The nostrils of his broad nose dilated and he murmured something to his wife.

With a long clothes-prop balanced on one thick, sloping shoulder, and clothes-pegs bulging in a sack slung over the other shoulder, Mr Samuels walked with a swaying gait on down-at-heel, faded boots. His brooding face carried the anxious story of his life and was of the coppery tint of velvety, dry magnolia leaves. On his massive head grew black hair, tinged with grey, and his greying moustache could not cover his wide, unfriendly mouth. Both he and his wife were returning from their work—Mr Samuels from selling props and pegs in back-yards and Mrs Samuels from washing clothes in a more prosperous suburb.

It occurred to me as they passed that I had never seen Mr Samuels talk to anyone in the street. He had no companions or friends in the neighbourhood, and he did not appear to want any. He barely acknowledged a greeting someone unexpectedly called to him.

While Mr Samuels was at home we children kept away and we pretended it was out of sympathy for Harry Johnson. Mr Samuels and his wife did not stir out of their house for several days, but as soon as they went to work again I began to hover round the doorstep where Lily sat after tea every evening.

I joined the Samuels children in a game of hopscotch on white squares drawn in chalk on the footpath. The white children playing at the other end of the street one by one came over to us. Even Harry Johnson watched from a distance.

I cast furtive glances at Lily, who sat hugging her knees and staring at the ground, and I was filled with a longing to sit next to her and talk to her. But I had suddenly become bashful. I could feel hot blood rushing into my face and neck. Awkwardly I tried to catch her eye, but she gave no sign.

I soon lost interest in the game and went and sat down on the edge of the footpath beside Charlie. Although he was my age I had never seen him play with anyone. He was now clutching tightly in his hands a punctured cardboard box that contained silkworms hidden in a bed of dark green mulberry leaves. He was completely absorbed with the precious worms and the problem of where to get more leaves for them. There was some sort of tree growing in a near-by back-yard and Charlie suggested we climb the fence and get some of its leaves.

"When it gets dark," I said weakly, averting my eyes from his sulky face.

Beyond the rise the sun had set in a fading, lilac-tinted sky and darkness overtook the moon still loitering behind the buildings and factories of the city. Here and there newly-lit kerosene lamps flickered through open windows. Down the street came strident shouts from a group of youths.

I remained seated, but Charlie rose impatiently and without a word disappeared down a dark side-lane leading to a back-yard. The voices of the youths came nearer. I saw them watching every movement of Lily's body as she rose from the doorstep. She must have been aware of their glances, for she became animated and a light tremor shook her angular figure.

"Hullo, Lil," they said. "Doing anything tonight?"

The three youths vied with each other for Lily's interest. I wondered what Mr Johnson would have thought, for his eldest son, Bert, was one of the three. But it was Tommy Jamieson who seemed to hold Lily's attention. He talked boastfully of his adventures in the city while the others sniggered sheepishly. Lily hardly spoke but her eyes sparkled mischievously and bashfully.

The orange moon had lifted itself from behind the city when mothers began to call their children home. The footpath became deserted except for the group near the doorway and myself sitting on the kerb. Even Lily's sisters and brothers had gone inside. A languid stillness crept over the street and Lily and the boys talked in whispers.

"Let's get away from here. Let's go for a walk," Tommy Jamieson said.

"Can't leave them on their own," she pointed with one thumb over her shoulder. "Dad and Mum aren't home yet."

"We'll get back before they come home," Tommy said, bending towards her. Then he turned to his companions and winked hard without looking at them.

Her gaze was misty and distant.

"Just to the corner," she said.

She walked hesitantly, followed by the youths, who had broken into a self-conscious swagger. On the corner she turned and gazed back at the two-story building that seemed cut out of the silvery, moonlit sky. A muffled conversation took place and then they continued towards the avenue on the rise ahead.

I was seized by a strange, unholy curiosity and I followed them at a discreet distance. Suddenly I heard soft, rustling footsteps behind me, and out of the corner of my eye I caught a glimpse of Charlie running in the shadows under the trees that grew on the edge of the footpath. But I was so possessed with curiosity that I hastened my steps and pretended that I hadn't seen him. Forgotten were my mother's warnings against going far afield at night, or her anxieties at my absence from home.

I waited anxiously to cross the busy, well-lit avenue. Far off the reddish gleam of the city's lights lay on the sky and the noise from the city mingled with the jangle of tram bells. For a moment I had lost sight of Lily and the boys, but soon I saw them turning into a street that ended in the park.

I ran into the park, peered round, and listened for the familiar voices. Overhead the dark trees sighed, creaked, and rustled as if turning in their beds. The bitter-sweet scent of gum-trees filled the air and the moon cast shafts of soft light that cleaved silvery passages through the darkness. I saw Lily sitting on a bench between two of the boys, while Tommy Jamieson sat on his heels at her feet. I crept closer and hid behind a tree.

"Let's sit on the grass," I heard Tommy say, while he idly fingered pebbles on the path.

Lily shook her head and giggled.

Suddenly Tommy rose to his feet, and catching hold of Lily's hand easily pulled her from the bench. She drew back and caught hold of the bench, but he put his arm round her waist and dragged her across the grass towards a big, spreading tree. She still struggled to free herself from his embrace, but he suddenly picked her up and falling on his knees brought her to the ground.

"Go easy, Tommy," said Bert Johnson nervously.

There was no reply from Tommy who was wildly pressing his lips against her face.

His companions looked round anxiously and then stared as if bewitched at the struggling pair. Lily's dress was pulled back revealing her slender, smooth brown thighs and legs.

Lily screamed.

"Leave her alone," Bert said urgently.

"Shut up," muttered Tommy through clenched teeth. "Who's she, anyway? She came with us, didn't she?"

"There's someone coming," Bert said fearfully. "Let's clear out." He stooped to tug at Tommy's coat.

I too had heard footsteps on the grass. Then I saw Charlie and his father hurrying in our direction.

Tommy scrambled to his feet.

"What are you frightened of?" he jeered at his two companions.

His words suddenly broke off as Mr Samuels and Charlie stumbled against them. Lily still lay on the ground crying angrily, and pulling her dress over her knees.

Muttering furiously in a thick voice Mr Samuels sent Tommy flying to the ground and kicked Bert Johnson in the stomach. He ran towards Tommy who was rising dazedly to his feet. In a fury he threw him down on the grass again and kicked him cruelly. When he seemed to have no strength to do more, he walked over to Lily and silently waited for her to rise. She struggled to her feet, averting her eyes from her father.

I was still trembling when they left the park, Charlie and his father on either side of Lily. I watched them get smaller in the distance and dissolve into the darkness. I cast a last glance at the boys. They were huddled together, Tommy supported by his two friends.

A frightening silence descended on the park. The shrunken moon had sailed high into the sky. Round me the trees stood like rigid sentries, their lips sealed. A feeling of mingled guilt and shame swept through me. Not only Bert Johnson and Tommy Jamieson were to blame, but in some way I too.

Then I remembered that I was long overdue at home, and I ran, my heart heavy with guilty secrets.

# NEAR THE WHARVES

A COLD, grey June evening had settled upon our street and sharp, biting air moved through the houses. They huddled together, silent, blinds drawn as if to shut out the winter.

In the distance buildings lost all shape and dissolved into darkness. Here and there a misty lamp shone from the summit of a tall post upon the empty, lifeless pavements.

Soon rain fell, a rain that stung and chilled; a dense curtain of water, a wall of taut threads.

I stood under the veranda of our house and gazed at the impatient and choking torrents that swept down ruts, hollows, and gutters, overflowed and flooded the street. I looked up. Two men were coming down towards me from the direction of the city. One was a stranger; the other was Mr Finnan, who lived across the way.

There was something strange about him. He walked unsteadily on the edge of the footpath and seemed barely able to lift his feet, while the stranger caught hold of his arm as if to prevent him from stumbling on the road. His oilskin coat fluttered in shreds and his trousers were torn and caked with mud and he was bare-headed. I wondered why he was without his undented, round hat that he always wore shoved far back from his forehead.

As the men passed our house helpless bursts of wheezy coughs followed one another out of Mr Finnan's convulsed body. With his grey, sagging face, hollow temples, and dark rings under his eyes he was awful to look at. From his head and coat rain fell in slanting lines to the ground.

"Hullo, Mr Finnan," I called.

He glanced in my direction but his eyes were misty and remote.

"Hullo, boy," he said in a far-away, hollow voice. Although he had spoken I was sure he hadn't seen me. Then as he passed I saw that the back of his head was a mingled mass of hair and blood.

I was horrified, and no sooner had the two men disappeared from sight than my mind filled with pictures of what might have happened to Mr Finnan. I saw him trampled by bolting horses, beset by larrikins. There were many bands of larrikins in our neighbourhood but on such an evening why should they leave their firesides to attack Mr Finnan?

When I lay down to sleep that night my thoughts were still on him. They were divided between a troubled pity for him and an intense curiousity as to what had overtaken him. In a dream I saw an empty street and slumped in the centre lay Mr Finnan bleeding from his head. Possessed with a feeling of shame and fear I stood fixed to my place in the street. We were alone in this great wilderness of houses and lamp-posts and I was unable to assist him. I turned over in my bed and awakening caught the sound of my own frightened cry.

Outside the window the morning had appeared. Rays of yellow light filtered through the cracks in the dark-green blind. The sound of metal-shod boots resounded on the cobbled lane outside my window. I groped for my clothes while my heart pounded swiftly. Fancy dreaming that I wouldn't go to Mr Finnan's assistance!

I was serious and silent at breakfast. Nor was Father as buoyant as usual. He barely glanced at me and he ate uninterestedly. Dipping his spoon into the bowl of sweetened bread and milk, he raised it almost to his mouth and then put it back into the bowl again.

"I haven't got an appetite," he said to Mother. Wiping his red moustache he stared glumly at the flower-patterned table-cloth.

"What's the use of my going out?" he burst out. "Nobody's got bottles to sell and what's the use of going to the country? My horse would only get bogged in the mud."

"A golden land," Mother said ironically. "You'll soon be unemployed, too."

"That would make everybody in the street equal," Father replied, staring fixedly at a nail in the wall, "except for that Mr Finnan and he's on strike."

"Some people have courage," Mother said.

Her words greatly offended Father and he said angrily, "You don't know how much courage it needs to go into back-yards where you're not wanted."

I left them arguing and when I got outside the street was shining with rain but the sky was dry and patches of blue peeped through white, slaty clouds. Near Mr Finnan's house some boys stood round the outskirts of a group of men.

Ignoring the boys I moved closer to the men and strained my ears to catch a word about Mr Finnan. The faces of the men were serious and pinched with the cold and they spoke softly. But the voice of Mr Dickenson rose above the others. He was a short, thick-set man of middle age and a sugar-bag full of vegetables rested at his feet. He did some casual work at the markets in the early hours of the morning, rising in pitch darkness, long before the fowls. For his work he was paid in potatoes, pumpkins, and cabbages. His deep-set, nimble eyes glittered knowingly.

"They haven't got a hope," he said. "They got the scabs in on the wharf yesterday. I knew they would."

"Finnan's a fool for getting mixed up in it,"said Mr Neil rubbing his knobbly, rheumatic hands together. He was an elderly man with a scowl permanently etched into his face

Another in the group shook his head in disagreement as he meditatively rolled a thin cigarette and after a moment's thought licked the paper. He was a grey-haired young invalid pensioner who had once been buried in a mine accident. His grey, threadbare coat held together by one button, flapped loosely.

"You wouldn't want him to stand with his hands in his pockets while the scabs took his job away," he said in a halting voice.

I lost the rest of the conversation. One of the boys tugged at my coat and called me to come away and play football. I shook my head impatiently; I couldn't leave the men, for I was deeply concerned about Mr Finnan's fate. But as if to hide from the temptation of the game going on behind me, I sidled into the centre of the group of men.

There was a silence when I mustered enough courage to ask, "What happened to Mr Finnan last night?"

"A policeman hit him on the head," Mr Dickenson said, tapping the top of his head with one finger. "And if you ask too many questions a policeman will hit you on the head," he added with a serious expression.

"Why don't you run away and play?" asked Mr Neil irritably.

"Get!" said Mr Dickenson.

My face became hot with embarrassment and I was angry with the men for laughing at me. Lest I should betray my agitation overmuch I delayed a few minutes, first pretending to examine my boots and then gazing around with a dignified air as if nothing had been said to me at all.

In the distance I saw the boys running down the street throwing and kicking the ball to each other. I knew they were going to the park and I envied them. The day had brightened up; it was almost mild and the sun occasionally peeped from behind grey cloud masses. The leaves of a near-by tree were gay with tiny, tired raindrops and the rays of fickle sunlight slanted through the leaves to the wet pavement.

Scraping my feet noisily I moved away from the men and sulkily lounged up against Mr Finnan's fence. With impotent anger I fiddled with an elastic shanghai that I drew out of my pocket. I was too afraid to fire it at the men and not one of the many cats and dogs in our street came within my range.

My black mood only passed away when Mrs Finnan came from her front door and walked to the gate. She was very thin and short and had wound a dark, woollen shawl around her shoulders. Although her face was drawn and her eyes sunken and tired with lack of sleep she was neat and tidy, as always. Her newly arranged grey, cork-screw curls bobbed with every step she took.

"How's Ned this morning, Mrs Finnan?" Mr Dickenson called to her, and respectfully tipped the peak of his cap.

"He's still a mess. He's got awful pains in his head."

The men came nearer.

"Is there anything we can do?" they asked.

"I don't know that you can do anything," she replied. "If he doesn't get better by this afternoon I'll take him back to the hospital."

"I didn't know that he'd been to the hospital," Mr Dickenson said in a shocked voice.

Mrs Finnan said, "A mate of his took him there after he was hit. But he wouldn't stay. Ned says to me, 'It's nothing but a butcher's shop! I don't want them messing about with me.' So as soon as he can he gets off the table and he comes home with his mate. He wanted to stay with him all night but I shooed him off. 'I can look after Ned', I said to him. We never got a wink of sleep, though. Ned vomited all night."

Mr Dickenson stirred uneasily. With two grimy fingers he rubbed his unshaven chin.

"Ned's game," he said slowly. "But what's the use?"

Mrs Finnan looked at him swiftly with angry eyes.

"You're not so game, are you, Mr Dickenson?" she said.

The grey-haired young pensioner intervened.

"How's Ned off for a smoke?" he asked diffidently, taking out his cigarette papers and shiny tin.

"He'll manage all right," she answered, waving the tobacco-tin away.

But later that day Mother sent me with a bowl of soup for Mr Finnan. Although she had never spoken to him she was moved by his plight and while she busied herself at the stove she was reminded of great events in the old country. She recalled a strike in 1905. It was on the docks, too. I must mention it to Mr Finnan, she said.

With careful steps, my head bent over the bowl held tightly in both hands, I walked slowly into Mr Finnan's house. From his chair by the stove he greeted me with a smile. With the soup in my hands, I stood tongue-tied and stared at him until he beckoned me to put the bowl down. I was unable to shift my gaze from his head, now covered

with a flannel bandage. His wound was completely con
cealed and there was not a spot of blood on the bandage.

"It's good of your mother," he said. "You thank her for
me. But I'm getting better now. The pain's about gone."

I nodded my head and awkwardly I stepped back to the
door.

"I don't know your name," he called me back.

Shyly I pulled a chair towards him and sat stiffly on the
edge of it. He asked me about my people. He never saw
them about much. He knew my father drove a bottle-cart.
Where did we come from? I gabbled my words. I explained
my mother couldn't speak the language; we kept to our own
people. All the time I talked, my mind was on his bandaged
head and I was eager to ask him about himself. But he
caught my attention when he told me that when he had
been a sailor he had travelled all over the world. He had
met people from every country. One day he would show
me his pictures of foreign ports.

I was overjoyed at his words and I was not surprised
that he had been a sailor. We boys had imagined that our
selves for we had once watched him paint the roof of his
house. Although he was tall and very thin and sallow, with
a narrow chest, his agility was extraordinary. He could
walk as easily on the roof as on the ground. His trousers
rolled up to his knees showing his lean, muscular legs, he
prowled over the roof like a bird. Only sailors could do that,
we had said.

Unconsciously I assumed an attitude of easy familiarity
and soon I was asking him about the fight on the water-
front. I was sure he could use his fists as all good sailors
must and I wanted to know how many opponents he had

laid out. But to my disappointment he made light of his part in the affair.

"It's all in the game," he said. "I'd like to meet your people some time," he added in a friendly voice.

I rose to go, my heart full of sympathy for him. With a sideways glance at him I said, "Do you want me to run a message or anything?"

"Well, would you like to take a note for me to Joe Tooley at the Union Hall?" he answered hesitantly.

I nodded my head eagerly.

He stood up and took from the mantelpiece an envelope and sheet of paper. The effort of rising appeared to affect him and he suppressed a sigh as he sat down. He scribbled a note and, sealing the envelope, told me how to find the Union Hall near the wharves.

"Joe's a mate of mine," he said. "Don't forget to tell him I'm better and I'll be down at the hall tomorrow." Then he added wryly, "Mrs Finnan wouldn't let me out today. She won't want me to go tomorrow, but I've got to go."

He stared down at his feet and deliberately began to roll himself a cigarette. His fingers trembled and he sprinkled the tobacco over his knees and I suddenly understood that he was in pain.

I hurried down the street with Mr Finnan's message. But on the way through the markets I began to dawdle. I was diverted by the bustle and noise round the stalls. I stopped and listened to the cries of the vendors and I fingered the three pennies in my pocket but decided against spending them just then.

Reluctantly moving on past the last market stalls, I reached the wharves on the river. From behind high galvanized-iron fences rose the tops of cranes and the masts of ships. They seemed to touch the black spidery clouds that hung from the grey, hard sky. I stopped to watch from a half-opened gate the unloading of a boat and I screwed up my eyes to read the name on the stern.

I had taken no notice of the policeman strolling round on the wharf until I heard a bystander behind me say that the ship was being worked by scabs. Then I recalled what I had to do. I felt in my pocket for Mr Finnan's letter and, re-assured by the crackle of paper, went off in search of the Union Hall. It was getting late and I had to be home before tea.

At last I stood in front of the hall and stared at the entrance blocked with men all talking animatedly. For a moment or so I wanted to run from these unfamiliar, noisy surroundings but I remembered my duty to Mr Finnan. I slowly edged my way through the crowd into a corridor out of which many rooms opened.

All round me there were men in working clothes. There was a smell of damp cloth and sodden boot leather and stale smoke and a blue haze hung like a cloud over the darkening corridor. An elderly man who held some papers in his hand came towards me. He spoke good-naturedly, "Who are you looking for, sonny?"

"Can you tell me where I can find Mr Tooley?" I asked.

"Joe Tooley?"

"Joe Tooley. That's him," I replied.

"He was pinched this afternoon," he said, watching me with a quizzical expression on his deeply creased face.

"Pinched," I said in a frightened voice.

"You Joe Tooley's boy?" the old man asked gently.

"No," I said. "Mr Finnan sent me to give him a letter."

"Well, you tell Ned that we'll get Joe out. He needn't worry."

I ran from the Union Hall as if pursued by the police myself. All my mother's dread of police asserted itself in me and I felt as if I had committed a crime. Never was I so glad to reach my own street. The light that shone in Mr Finnan's window gave me back a little of that feeling of security that had deserted me through the city's streets.

There was a homely smell of cooking in the kitchen and there I told Mr Finnan that Joe Tooley was in jail. Straightening his stooped shoulders he leaned back in his chair and said, "That's funny. We were joking about quod only yesterday. Well, I'll see him tomorrow."

Mrs Finnan glanced sharply at him from under puffy eyelids.

"You can't go anywhere tomorrow. Have some sense, Ned. You're still sick."

"All right, all right, we won't talk about it now," he said, and brought the conversation to an end.

A misty rain greeted me the next morning when I came out to the veranda to farewell Father as he drove away in search of bottles and bags. Across the way I saw Mr Finnan with a group of people. All of them faced Mrs Finnan, who was behind the gate.

As I approached them Mr Dickenson was talking.

"I wish I was as certain as you, Ned," he was saying. "Things don't look too good to me."

Mr Neil interrupted him. "You'll only be getting yourself run in too if you're not careful."

He avoided Mr Finnan's eyes and scowled at the boys who played round the men. Mr Finnan smoked and smiled, but the frown furrowing his forehead stirred heavily. His face was ashen and his long, thin frame was stooped as if a heavy stone rested on his shoulders. An old crumpled hat sat squarely on top of his bandaged head.

"If I listened to you I'd let my mates down. Anyway, what are you worried about? You've got a lot to be thankful for, haven't you?" He started to walk away.

"You're not well enough to be going out today, Ned," Mr Dickenson called solemnly after him.

"That's what I said," burst out Mrs Finnan, her face smaller and sharper than ever.

Mr Finnan stopped and turned to face us.

"I've never felt better in my life," he boasted. "I haven't got any reason for stopping home."

"Won't there be more trouble today?" Mr Dickenson asked.

Mr Finnan shrugged his shoulders as though astonished at the stupidity of the question. Then he waved to his wife.

"I'll walk along with you, Ned," said the young grey-haired pensioner. His loose coat held together by one solitary button, hung awkwardly like the broken wing of a bird.

Meanwhile I was boasting to the boys that I knew Mr Finnan was going to get his mate, Joe Tooley, out of jail. I knew how he was going to do it, but I couldn't let anyone else into that secret. Not to be outdone, they boasted of the things they had done while I was away at the Union Hall. We bickered until Mrs Finnan spoke again to the men who still stood around her gate.

"I've got a donkey for a husband," she said bitterly, "that's what I've got. A donkey. He won't take notice of anybody. He should be in bed."

"That's what I think, Mrs Finnan," said Mr Dickenson in an ingratiating voice.

She puckered her face and shot a venomous glance at him.

"So that's what you think?" she said angrily. "You seem to have a lot to say for yourself. With your tongue, you could be doing something to help them instead of standing there like a frozen statue."

Casting a haughty glance at the men, with a quick movement she pulled her shawl tightly around herself, sniffed the air with her thin nostrils, stiffened her back and walked hurriedly towards the open door of her house.

The men avoided each others' eyes. It was only then they seemed to realize that it was a raw, bleak morning. Silently they disappeared from the street. A misty rain began to fall from the grey-yellow sky. We boys continued to bicker and argue.

# MAKING A LIVING

Another journey. But this time we went on holidays. Well, not exactly holidays, but something near enough.

It was the summer after I had my thirteenth birthday and Father said, "If we don't get out of the city for a while we'll starve like dogs in an orphanage."

Father's affairs were going badly again; bottle dealing was worse than bad, nobody bought bottles and no one had any to sell. Times were hard.

So Father had become a horse-dealer. He bought a few horses and all the would-be buyers yawned, scratched themselves, looked sideways and said, "Things are bad. We'll do with the horses we've got."

And those buyers who could afford more horses as soon as they set eyes on Father's decided to go in for motor-cars instead. When Father took up horse-dealing motor-cars were becoming popular. Honestly, evil fortune followed Father like a faithful hound.

Father sat about the house for days and puzzled the whole matter out. He had an idea. He would take several of his horses to the outskirts of the city and let them loose—they would finish up in a municipal pound. But his two best-looking horses could still be put to some use. He would take them to a holiday resort where he would hire them out as riding hacks to timid holiday-makers.

The more Father thought of his plan the more intoxicated he became with it and he was convinced that the timid holiday-makers were waiting for just these two horses.

And of course there were many other things Father could do at the holiday resort.

Thus was born a second idea to Father. He would drive his cart round the hills buying rabbit skins and hides and tallow and what-not, while I would be responsible for the two horses, hiring them out at the guest-houses, the hotels, and in the street. After all, why shouldn't I help in making a living for the family? I was no longer a child. I had a tongue and a pair of hands. What harm would it do my mind? Father asked with passion.

Without looking at him Mother replied, "I always said our son would have to struggle here just as I did back home. I knew it from the first day we landed in this golden kingdom."

But despite Mother's words I was elated that it fell to me to help the family in such hard times. I could see no reason for her unhappy reflections. I felt like the other boys in the street and all of them had to do something for their families. Some of them had begun to work years ago.

Father's plan mapped out, every detail well cared for, off we went to Berrigullen, the fashionable holiday place in the hills. In such a resort Father said even if we only ate dry bread it would still be a holiday for all of us. Why, even the air in Berrigullen was noted for its wonders—it was said that the old became young, the sick healthy, and more besides. That was why so many important people in our community were beginning to go there for their holidays.

We locked up our house and loaded the spring-cart with blankets, pots and pans, saddles, spare sets of harness, three black hens, a white rooster and a part fox-terrier that, properly speaking, belonged to the whole street. The two horses that for a change were going to help feed us were tied by halters to the back of the cart.

The street turned out to see us off. Friends, acquaintances, neighbours came out of their houses as though to watch a funeral or a brawl. Some of them stood on their verandas and waved to us. And as there were many men out of work at the time, a large crowd of people of all ages stood round the cart, laughing, gossiping, giving friendly advice, and wishing us good fortune.

It was a warm send-off, but Father was filled with gloom and his pale-blue eyes were dull and sad as though with pain. He had hardly spoken a word. He nodded his head absent-mindedly and stared unseeingly at the neighbourly men and women and barefooted children.

"Ah, these accursed journeys," he suddenly whispered to me, "and for what?"

His voice was filled with such sorrow that it seemed to me Father had suddenly seen through all his dreams and schemes and his heart had emptied at the prospect before him at the end of this new journey. I understood then how much Father had always hated moving.

I felt with him and I was fretful at leaving the neighbourhood. As we drove off and I waved to my companions I envied each one of them. There were Tom and Joe and Benny, and I thought of everything they would do this day—the stories they would tell each other, the games they would play, the walks through city lanes and streets.

My peevishness grew as we jogged through miles and miles of suburbs. Everywhere bystanders gazed in our direction. What was it they were looking at? Was it that the harness on the chestnut drawing our cart was threadbare and held together with wire and string, and that tufts of yellow straw stuck out of the collar? Or was it because one wheel of the cart wobbled alarmingly?

I knew it was neither. The people were looking at us. That was nothing new, for we were frequently stared at when we drove through suburban streets. But now it was different. Everything affronted me—the handsome respectable houses, the broad clean streets, the complacent, healthy faces of the people so different from those we had left behind. My irritation grew into anger when a group of men and women looked at us a little too long. There was something ironical about their gaze and one woman pointed with amusement to the two horses jogging resignedly behind the cart.

"What are you staring at?" I shouted at them. Then I picked up an empty bottle from the floor of the cart and I threw it at the group where it crashed into splinters at their feet.

Mother, startled out of her reverie, glanced in the direction of the people gesticulating at us. Then she looked at me angrily.

"Why did you behave like a hooligan?" she demanded.

I was stubbornly silent and she repeated her question. I refused to speak, it would have been impossible to explain why I had thrown the bottle. If I could have done so she might have understood and perhaps she would have ceased her bitter and ironical musings.

She said, "You remain silent. I think I understand why. We hardly speak a common language any more. You belong to one world, I belong to another. With your new ways you have almost become a stranger to me." And then she asked in her gentlest voice, "Please tell me one thing—where did you acquire the cultured habit of throwing bottles at strangers?"

She went on and on but Father said nothing. He was absorbed in his own thoughts but for some reason I felt that he secretly understood my behaviour. Perhaps I had in some way expressed his feelings, too.

We were all silent when we drove into the main street of Berrigullen. We were all too moody and far away to take in the beauty of the surroundings. The township was like a garden with its rows of poplars and elms and the fruit-trees that hung over fences and hedges. On all sides in the distance tier upon tier of hills rent the fading blue sky and walled in Berrigullen.

It was not in the main street or on the heights that we lived. We had a furnished cottage in a hollow below the township where seldom any traffic passed; the sound of voices in that neighbourhood almost created a sensation.

There was an unfriendly look about our new house and at night the paper pasted over the chinks of the windows sounded in the breeze like the patter of frightened feet. It was the last cottage on the road and the bush came right up to the side fence and the back-yard was overgrown with bracken. Half a mile down the road a row of cottages similar to ours stood close to each other. There were no holiday-makers in those dwellings. There lived old-age pensioners, rabbit trappers, and fruit pickers.

I had no time to explore round the houses on our road, I had work to do. The day after we arrived in Berrigullen I was to take the two horses into the township, stand near the hotel or one of the guest-houses, preferably the biggest and best and get clients, the timid holiday-makers who were waiting for our two mounts. Father explained everything, what I was to say and how I was to say it. Apparently satisfied that I should be successful, he drove away into the hills.

Saddled and ready to be ridden, the horses ambled behind me up the steep track towards the main street. From a distance some boys called to me but I ignored them. How were they to know that I was on a most important mission? It was the first time I had taken any part in the making of a living for the family and nothing would divert me. I dreamt of the money I would bring home. In my mind I counted my earnings over and over again. I could see the coins stacked on the kitchen table so that even Mother would have to admit that she was wrong and that Father was not foolish in sending me to hire out the horses. I was filled with pride and everything round me quickened my elated feelings—the summer morning, the sweet scent of gums, the hum of insects, the cries of birds, the hot, still air. How wonderful everything seemed just then!

But as soon as I was in the main street my elation began to ebb and I saw my task in a more sombre light. Slyly fear and shame had crept into me. Where would I start? I looked round at the large houses with trees and flower bushes hiding from sight the doors and windows, and I wondered if they were the guest-houses from which I should get my customers. To make matters worse, all the words Father had carefully impressed on me vanished from my mind. I had forgotten what to say and what to do.

In despair I walked the horses up the street and then back again. The two steeds were resigned to their fate and their heads drooped in philosophical contemplation, like wise parrots in a cage.

I stopped when children's voices floated towards me from the lawn of a long, rambling house that I rightly believed must be a fashionable guest-house. In a moment I made up my mind, walked over to the gate and tied the horses to a telegraph post. Behind the low fence boys and girls played, while well-dressed men and women sat on garden benches under trees, some reading, others just chatting.

I scanned the faces of the men and women and I recognized Mr Frumkin and his wife. They were well known to me, particularly Mr Frumkin, with whom Father had for so long dealt. He was now the leading dealer in the bottle business while his wife was a notable in various ladies' societies in our community. They sat stiffly and silently and neither of them smiled or waved back to me when I shouted cheerfully, "Hullo, Mr and Mrs Frumkin!"

And, imagining that they might be interested in my doings, I called again, "I've got two horses here I want to hire out."

They shifted their gaze and stared down at their feet.

For a moment I was bewildered, but the snub from the Frumkins in some unexpected way gave me strength and entirely restored my faded confidence. I thought of how I could increase their discomfiture and then I remembered the purpose for which I was outside the gate of the guest-house.

Swaggering slightly I called to the guests on the garden seats, "Who wants to hire a good horse? Only a bob an hour."

Nobody rose from his seat. Here and there an amused smile, a haughty stare; even the children went on with their playing. Several boys made as though to come over to me but they were stopped by the grown-ups.

I continued to call my wares as though at the market. Even there one had to shout and shout to attract customers —sooner or later someone must come over.

Without a glance in my direction the Frumkin couple left their seats and made for the veranda of the guest-house. I called insolently to Mr Frumkin. "What about you, Mr Frumkin? The horse's back is wide enough for your behind."

There were a few sniggers and, needing little encouragement, I continued to shout at the Frumkin couple until they disappeared into the house. Then I went on again with my business cries. Soon a man came up to the gate and he stared at me severely.

I looked him up and down and said, "You can have your pick. Only a bob an hour."

His face went crimson.

"Clear out," he said angrily. "Nobody wants your horses. Get!" he added furiously.

I edged back slowly towards the horses.

"What if I don't get?" I said.

"I'll see that you do," he said menacingly.

"Well, I'm not going for you, anyway," I said and turned to the guests, who had risen from their seats at the commotion.

"Who wants to hire a good horse? Only a bob an hour!" I shouted at them and out of the corner of my eye I watched the menacing gentleman.

He made as though to open the gate, and with a sudden onrush of rage, I stooped down and picked up a handful of stones. I held them in my clenched fist, ready to throw the lot at him should he but go past the gate. He stared intently at me as though to judge how serious my intentions were. He must have been quite satisfied, for he turned abruptly on his heels and walked back to the guests who were strolling towards the gate. He said something to them as he passed and they, like sheep, followed him until they all disappeared. Only a few boys remained on the lawn playing with a bat and ball.

I put my thumb to my nose and shouted derisively at them. Then, with exaggerated slowness I took the horses down the road again. There and then I decided I would have nothing more to do with guest-houses. As I passed one after another it seemed to me they were all the same, with their stiff lines and their hard, suspicious exteriors. Perhaps I attributed to the buildings something that rightly belonged to the people sitting on the well-kept lawns.

The horses stopped to drink from a trough near the hotel. The air was hot and still in the broad, sleepy road. Across the way a store rested drowsily in the shade of two poplars and the creek behind murmured gently. Overhead green and red and yellow rosellas flew with a faint hissing noise from tree to tree.

I tethered the horses to posts and walked to the veranda of the hotel. Under the open windows of the bar-room two old men sat without speaking to each other. They looked as if they were part of the wooden bench and from their ancient, shiny serge suits I guessed they were natives of the township and not holiday-makers.

One of them was idly drawing his stick over the floor and both looked up at me with expectant eyes, as though glad of any diversion.

"Do you think anyone in the hotel wants to hire a horse— cheap?" I asked.

"Well, I don't know, sonny," one of them said. "There's a riding school here and, besides, the hotel's got a few hacks."

"My horses would be as good as the others," I said.

"I wouldn't know," the old man replied and winked slyly at his companion.

He, with a faint grin wrinkling his face, screwed up his eyes and with the air of an expert gazed at the two horses.

"They look good horses to me," he said. "Not as young as they used to be and a bit short of wind, but I can see they've been good workers."

I walked with firm steps into the bar, believing my horses vouched for by two old men, and I spoke with a full heart to the men standing at the damp, glistening counter.

"I've got the best two horses in Berrigullen for hire. Wonderful to ride and only a bob an hour."

The drinkers turned around slowly and looked at me with lazy eyes. One of them said, "We've got no time for riding."

There was laughter at his words and another man said, "Come and have a drink, lad. Lemonade, eh?"

I stood up against the counter and imitating the men I held my glass of lemonade as jauntily as they held their beer. I pushed my cap back and sipped my drink slowly as I looked around the bar. On the walls and above the shelves laden with bottles there were framed pictures of horses, boxers, and footballers. Some of them were familiar to me, others were heroes of before my time.

I could make neither head nor tail of the conversation that continued around me. There were jokes about a party that had been held in the hotel the night before. And there was talk about hang-overs and how they should be cured. I was afraid to finish my lemonade, thinking that so long as I was in the bar I still had a chance of finding at least one customer.

I turned to the man who had bought me the lemonade.

I said, "Wouldn't you like a ride on one of the horses?"

He looked at me humorously and then put a shilling in my hand. Without a word he joined in the conversation again.

I gazed sheepishly at the shilling until the barman leaned over and, tapping me on the shoulder, pointed his thumb at the door. I hastily gulped the rest of my drink and walked out into the sunlight, my face red with the knowledge that the barman had thought I was a beggar. I was ashamed to look the two old men in the face.

"No luck?" one of them asked sympathetically.

The other said, "Those blokes in there never ride horses. They spend all their time drinking. You went to the wrong place, sonny."

"You'll never make anything out of those blokes," the first old man said. "They're takers, not givers."

I suppose the old men knew all about the holiday-makers in the hotel for they sat on the wooden bench all day. But it didn't console me and my heart was heavy when I went back to the horses and led them across the road so that they could nibble at the tufts of grass under the trees.

I blindly reproached myself with my failure and I felt guilty about my behaviour at the guest-house. I had one shilling to show for all my effort and I clutched it as if afraid that even it might fly away. Sitting on the edge of the road I stared disconsolately ahead. Only the two old men were to be seen and they looked at me with faraway eyes as if constantly turning over their memories. Silence lay over the township and the sun shone down on the rust red gravel with a fiery brilliance.

I rose from the ground to take my charges back home. The two sleepy, timid horses were stuck to me like a tail and they were my responsibility until I could return them to Father.

The main street, the guest-houses, the hotel disappeared from my sight as we descended the steep track. Nothing could now elate me. Around me was just lonely bush, grey trees and blackberry-bushes encroaching on both sides of the track. Behind the horses dust rose in tiny clouds and rolled away towards the trees. I felt my face. It was covered with dust and my fingers were black and sticky.

When I reached the bottom of the hill near our house I stopped by a tree and watched the horses nibble happily at the dry brown leaves on the ground. I couldn't face my mother just yet. I had suddenly become afraid of her intent searching eyes, her bitter words. Something had happened to me this day that would want thinking out. For the first time I had stepped out into the world and I had touched with my own hands the hard kernel of life, getting a living.

## MOTHER

WHEN I was a small boy I was often morbidly conscious of Mother's intent, searching eyes fixed on me. She would gaze for minutes on end without speaking one word. I was always disconcerted and would guiltily look down at the ground, anxiously turning over in my mind my day's activities.

But very early I knew her thoughts were far away from my petty doings; she was concerned with them only in so far as they gave her further reason to justify her hostility to the life around us. She was preoccupied with my sister and me; she was for ever concerned with our future in this new land in which she would always feel a stranger.

I gave her little comfort, for though we had been in the country for only a short while I had assumed many of the ways of those around me. I had become estranged from her. Or so it seemed to Mother, and it grieved her.

When I first knew her she had no intimate friend, nor do I think she felt the need of one with whom she could discuss her innermost thoughts and hopes. With me, though I knew she loved me very deeply, she was never on such near terms of friendship as sometimes exist between a mother and son. She emanated a kind of certainty in herself, in her view of life, that no opposition or human difficulty could shrivel or destroy. "Be strong before people, only weep before God," she would say and she lived up to that precept even with Father.

In our little community in the city, acquaintances spoke derisively of Mother's refusal to settle down as others had done, of what they called her propensity for highfalutin day-dreams and of the severity and unreasonableness of her opinions.

Yet her manner with people was always gentle. She spoke softly, she was measured in gesture, and frequently it seemed she was functioning automatically, her mind far away from her body. There was a grave beauty in her still, sad face, her searching, dark-brown eyes and black hair. She was thin and stooped in carriage as though a weight always lay on her shoulders.

From my earliest memory of Mother it somehow seemed quite natural to think of her as apart and other-worldly and different, not of everyday things as Father was. In those days he was a young-looking man who did not hesitate to make friends with children as soon as they were able to talk to him and laugh at his stories. Mother was older than he was. She must have been a woman of nearly forty, but she seemed even older. She changed little for a long time, showing no traces of growing older at all until, towards the end of her life, she suddenly became an old lady.

I was always curious about Mother's age. She never had birthdays like other people, nor did anyone else in our family. No candles were ever lit or cakes baked or presents given in our house. To my friends in the street who boasted of their birthday parties I self-consciously repeated my Mother's words, that such celebrations were only a foolish and eccentric form of self-worship.

"Nothing but deception," she would say. "As though life can be chopped into neat twelve-month parcels! It's deeds, not years, that matter."

Although I often repeated her words and even prided myself on not having birthdays I could not restrain myself from once asking Mother when she was born.

"I was born. I'm alive as you can see, so what more do you want to know?" she replied, so sharply that I never asked her about her age again.

In so many other ways Mother was different. Whereas all the rest of the women I knew in the neighbouring houses and in other parts of the city took pride in their housewifely abilities, their odds and ends of new furniture, the neat appearance of their homes, Mother regarded all those things as of little importance. Our house always looked as if we had just moved in or were about to move out. An impermanent and impatient spirit dwelt within our walls; Father called it living on one leg like a bird.

Wherever we lived there were some cases partly unpacked, rolls of linoleum stood in a corner, only some of the windows had curtains. There were never sufficient wardrobes, so that clothes hung on hooks behind doors. And all the time Mother's things accumulated. She never parted with anything, no matter how old it was. A shabby green plush coat bequeathed to her by her own mother hung on a nail in her bedroom. Untidy heaps of tattered books, newspapers, and journals from the old country mouldered in corners of the house, while under her bed in tin trunks she kept her dearest possessions. In those trunks there were bundles of old letters, two heavily underlined books on nursing, an old Hebrew Bible, three silver spoons given her by an aunt with whom she had once lived, a diploma on yellow parchment, and her collection of favourite books.

From one or other of her trunks she would frequently pick a book and read to my sister and me. She would read in a wistful voice poems and stories of Jewish liberators from Moses until the present day, of the heroes of the 1905 Revolution and pieces by Tolstoy and Gorki and Sholom Aleichem. Never did she stop to inquire whether we understood what she was reading; she said we should understand later if not now.

I liked to hear Mother read, but always she seemed to choose a time for reading that clashed with something or other I was doing in the street or in a near-by paddock. I would be playing with the boys in the street, kicking a football or spinning a top or flying a kite, when Mother would unexpectedly appear and without even casting a glance at my companions she would ask me to come into the house, saying she wanted to read to me and my sister. Sometimes I was overcome with humiliation and I would stand listlessly with burning cheeks until she repeated her words. She never reproached me for my disobedience nor did she ever utter a reproof to the boys who taunted me as, crestfallen, I followed her into the house.

Why Mother was as she was only came to me many years later. Then I was even able to guess when she was born.

She was the last child of a frail and overworked mother and a bleakly pious father who hawked reels of cotton and other odds and ends in the villages surrounding a town in Russia. My grandfather looked with great disapproval on his offspring, who were all girls, and he was hardly aware of my mother at all. She was left well alone by her older sisters, who with feverish impatience were waiting for their parents to make the required arrangements for their marriages.

During those early days Mother rarely looked out into the streets, for since the great pogroms few Jewish children were ever to be seen abroad. From the iron grille of the basement she saw the soles of the shoes of the passers-by and not very much more. She had never seen a tree, a flower, or a bird.

But when Mother was about fifteen her parents died and she went to live with a widowed aunt and her large family in a far-away village. Her aunt kept an inn and Mother was tucked away with her cousins in a remote part of the building, away from the prying eyes of the customers in the tap-rooms. Every evening her aunt would gaze at her with startled eyes as if surprised to find her among the family.

"What am I going to do with you?" she would say. "I've got daughters of my own. If only your dear father of blessed name had left you just a tiny dowry it would have been such a help. Ah well! If you have no hand you can't make a fist."

At that time Mother could neither read nor write. And as she had never had any childhood playmates or friends of any kind she hardly knew what to talk about with her cousins. She spent the days cheerlessly pottering about the kitchen or sitting for hours, her eyes fixed on the dark wall in front of her.

Some visitor to the house, observing the small, lonely girl, took pity on her and decided to give her an education. Mother was given lessons every few days and after a while she acquired a smattering of Yiddish and Russian, a little arithmetic, and a great fund of Russian and Jewish stories.

New worlds gradually opened before Mother. She was seized with a passion for primers, grammars, arithmetic and story books, and soon the idea entered her head that the way out of her present dreary life lay through these books. There was another world, full of warmth and interesting things, and in it there was surely a place for her. She became obsessed with the thought that it wanted only some decisive step on her part to go beyond her aunt's house into the life she dreamed about.

Somewhere she read of a Jewish hospital which had just opened in a distant city and one winter's night she told her aunt she wanted to go to relatives who lived there. They would help her to find work in the hospital.

"You are mad!" exclaimed her aunt. "Forsake a home for a wild fancy! Who could have put such a notion into your head? Besides, a girl of eighteen can't travel alone at this time of the year."

It was from that moment that Mother's age became something to be manipulated as it suited her. She said to her aunt that she was not eighteen, but twenty-two. She was getting up in years and she could not continue to impose on her aunt's kindness.

"How can you be twenty-two?" her aunt replied greatly puzzled.

A long pause ensued while she tried to reckon up Mother's years. She was born in the month Tammuz according to the Jewish calendar, which corresponded to the old-style Russian calendar month of June, but in what year? She could remember being told of Mother's birth, but nothing outstanding had happened then to enable her to place the year. With all her nieces and nephews, some dead and many alive, scattered all over the vastness of the country only a genius could keep track of all their birthdays. Perhaps the girl was twenty-two, and if that were so her chance of getting a husband in the village was pretty remote; twenty-two was far too old. The thought entered her head that if she allowed Mother to go to their kinsmen in the city she would be relieved of the responsibility of finding a dowry for her, and so reluctantly she agreed.

But it was not until the spring that she finally consented to let her niece go. As the railway station was several miles from the village Mother was escorted there on foot by her aunt and cousins. With all her possessions, including photographs of her parents and a tattered Russian primer tied in a great bundle, Mother went forth into the vast world.

In the hospital she didn't find that for which she hungered; it seemed still as far away as in the village. She had dreamed of the new life where all would be noble, where men and women would dedicate their lives to bringing about a richer and happier life, just as she had read.

But she was put to scrubbing floors and washing linen every day from morning till night until she dropped exhausted into her bed in the attic. No one looked at her, no one spoke to her but to give her orders. Her one day off in the month she spent with her relatives who gave her some cast-off clothes and shoes and provided her with the books on nursing she so urgently needed. She was more than ever convinced that her deliverance would come through these books and she set about swallowing their contents with renewed zest.

As soon as she had passed all the examinations and acquired the treasured diploma she joined a medical mission that was about to proceed without a moment's delay to a distant region where a cholera epidemic raged. And then for several years she remained with the same group, moving from district to district, wherever disease flourished.

Whenever Mother looked back over her life it was those years that shone out. Then she was with people who were filled with an ardour for mankind and it seemed to her they lived happily and freely, giving and taking friendship in an atmosphere pulsating with warmth and hope.

All this had come to an end in 1905 when the medical mission was dissolved and several of Mother's colleagues were killed in the uprising. Then with a heavy heart and little choice she had returned to nursing in the city, but this time in private houses attending on well-to-do ladies.

It was at the home of one of her patients that she met Father. What an odd couple they must have been! She was taciturn, choosing her words carefully, talking mainly of her ideas and little about herself. Father bared his heart with guileless abandon. He rarely had secrets and there was no division in his mind between intimate and general matters. He could talk as freely of his feelings for Mother or of a quarrel with his father as he could of a vaudeville show or the superiority of one game of cards as against another.

Father said of himself he was like an open hand at solo and all men were his brothers. For a story, a joke, or an apt remark he would forsake his father and mother, as the saying goes. Old tales, new ones invented for the occasion, jokes rolled off his tongue in a never-ending procession. Every trifle, every incident was material for a story and he haunted music-halls and circuses, for he liked nothing better than comedians and clowns, actors and buskers.

He brought something bubbly and frivolous into Mother's life and for a while she forgot her stern precepts. In those days Father's clothes were smart and gay; he wore bright straw hats and loud socks and fancy, buttoned-up boots. Although she had always regarded any interest in clothes as foolish and a sign of an empty and frivolous nature Mother then felt proud of his fashionable appearance. He took her to his favourite resorts, to music-halls and to tea-houses where he and his cronies idled away hours, boastfully recounting stories of successes in business or merely swapping jokes. They danced nights away, though Mother was almost stupefied by the band and the bright lights and looked with distaste on the extravagant clothes of the dancers who bobbed and cavorted.

All this was in the early days of their marriage. But soon Mother was filled with misgivings. Father's world, the world of commerce and speculation, of the buying and selling of goods neither seen nor touched, was repugnant and frightening to her. It lacked stability, it was devoid of ideals, it was fraught with ruin. Father was a trader in air, as the saying went.

Mother's anxiety grew as she observed more closely his mode of life. He worked in fits and starts. If he made enough in one hour to last him a week or a month his business was at an end and he went off in search of friends and pleasure. He would return to business only when his money had just about run out. He was concerned only with one day at a time; about tomorrow he would say, clicking his fingers, his blue eyes focused mellowly on space, "We'll see."

But always he had plans for making great fortunes. They never came to anything but frequently they produced unexpected results. It so happened that on a number of occasions someone Father trusted acted on the plans he had talked about so freely before he even had time to leave the tea-house. Then there were fiery scenes with his faithless friends. But Father's rage passed away quickly and he would often laugh and make jokes over the table about it the very same day. He imagined everyone else forgot as quickly as he did and he was always astonished to discover that his words uttered hastily in anger had made him enemies.

"How should I know that people have such long memories for hate? I've only a cat's memory," he would explain innocently.

"If you spit upwards, you're bound to get it back in the face," Mother irritably upbraided him.

Gradually Mother reached the conclusion that only migration to another country would bring about any real change in their life, and with all her persistence she began to urge him to take the decisive step. She considered America, France, Palestine, and finally decided on Australia. One reason for the choice was the presence there of distant relatives who would undoubtedly help them to find their feet in that far-away continent. Besides, she was sure that Australia was so different from any other country that Father was bound to acquire a new and more solid way of earning a living there.

For a long time Father paid no heed to her agitation and refused to make any move.

"Why have you picked on Australia and not Tibet, for example?" he asked ironically. "There isn't much difference between the two lands. Both are on the other side of the moon."

The idea of leaving his native land seemed so fantastic to him that he refused to regard it seriously. He answered

Mother with jokes and tales of travellers who disappeared in balloons. He had no curiosity to explore distant countries, he hardly ever ventured beyond the three or four familiar streets of his city. And why should his wife be so anxious for him to find a new way of earning a living? Didn't he provide her with food and a roof over her head? He had never given one moment's thought to his mode of life and he could not imagine any reason for doing so. It suited him like his gay straw hats and smart suits.

Yet in the end he did what Mother wanted him to do, though even on the journey he was tortured by doubts and he positively shouted words of indecision. But he was no sooner in Australia than he put away all thoughts of his homeland and he began to regard the new country as his permanent home. It was not so different from what he had known before. Within a few days he had met some fellow merchants and, retiring to a café, they talked about business in the new land. There were fortunes to be made here, Father very quickly concluded. There was, of course, the question of a new language but that was no great obstacle to business. You could buy and sell—it was a good land, Father said.

It was different with Mother. Before she was one day off the ship she wanted to go back.

The impressions she gained on that first day remained with her all her life. It seemed to her there was an irritatingly superior air about the people she met, the customs officials, the cab men, the agent of the new house. Their faces expressed something ironical and sympathetic, something friendly and at the same time condescending. She imagined everyone on the wharf, in the street, looked at her in the same way and she never forgave them for treating her as if she were in need of their good-natured tolerance.

Nor was she any better disposed to her relatives and the small delegation of Jews who met her at the ship. They had all been in Australia for many years and they were anxious to impress new-comers with their knowledge of the country and its customs. They spoke in a hectoring manner. This was a free country, they said, it was cultured, one used a knife and fork and not one's hands. Everyone could read and write and no one shouted at you. There were no oppressors here as in the old country.

Mother thought she understood their talk; she was quick and observant where Father was sometimes extremely guileless. While they talked Father listened with a good-natured smile and it is to be supposed he was thinking of a good story he could tell his new acquaintances. But Mother fixed them with a firm, relentless gaze and, suddenly interrupting their injunctions, said in the softest of voices, "If there are no oppressors here, as you say, why do you frisk about like house dogs? Whom do you have to please?"

Mother never lost this hostile and ironical attitude to the new land. She would have nothing of the country; she would not even attempt to learn the language. And she only began to look with a kind of interest at the world round her when my sister and I were old enough to go to school. Then all her old feeling for books and learning was re-awakened. She handled our primers and readers as if they were sacred texts.

She set great aims for us. We were to shine in medicine, in literature, in music; our special sphere depended on her fancy at a particular time. In one of these ways we could serve humanity best, and whenever she read to us the stories of Tolstoy and Gorki she would tell us again and again of her days with the medical mission. No matter how much schooling we should get we needed ideals, and what better ideals were there than those that had guided her in the days of the medical mission? They would save us from the soulless influences of this barren land.

Father wondered why she spent so much time reading and telling us stories of her best years and occasionally he would take my side when I protested against Mother taking us away from our games.

"They're only children," he said. "Have pity on them. If you stuff their little heads, God alone knows how they will finish up." Then, pointing to us, he added, "I'll be satisfied if he is a good carpenter; and if she's a good dressmaker that will do, too."

"At least," Mother replied, "you have the good sense not to suggest they go in for business. Life has taught you something at last."

"Can I help it that I am in business?" he suddenly shouted angrily. "I know it's a pity my father didn't teach me to be a professor."

But he calmed down quickly, unable to stand for long Mother's steady gaze and compressed lips.

It exasperated us that Father should give in so easily so that we could never rely on him to take our side for long. Although he argued with Mother about us he secretly agreed with her. And outside the house he boasted about her, taking a peculiar pride in her culture and attainments, and repeating her words just as my sister and I did.

Mother was very concerned about how she could give us a musical education. It was out of the question that we both be taught an instrument, since Father's business was at a low ebb and he hardly knew where he would find enough money to pay the rent, so she took us to a friend's house to listen to gramophone records. They were of the old-fashioned, cylindrical kind made by Edison and they sounded far away and thin like the voice of a ventriloquist mimicking far off musical instruments. But my sister and I marvelled at them. We should have been willing to sit over the long, narrow horn for days, but Mother decided that it would only do us harm to listen to military marches and the stupid songs of the music-hall.

It was then that we began to pay visits to musical emporiums. We went after school and during the holidays in the mornings. There were times when Father waited long for his lunch or evening meal, but he made no protest. He supposed Mother knew what she was doing in those shops and he told his friends of the effort Mother was making to acquaint us with music.

Our first visits to the shops were in the nature of reconnoitring sorties. In each emporium Mother looked the attendants up and down while we thumbed the books on the counters, stared at the enlarged photographs of illustrious composers, and studied the various catalogues of gramophone records. We went from shop to shop until we just about knew all there was to know about the records and sheet music and books in stock.

Then we started all over again from the first shop and this time we came to hear the records.

I was Mother's interpreter and I would ask one of the salesmen to play us a record she had chosen from one of the catalogues. Then I would ask him to play another. It might have been a piece for violin by Tchaikowsky or Beethoven or an aria sung by Caruso or Chaliapin. This would continue until Mother observed the gentleman in charge of the gramophone losing his patience and we would take our leave.

With each visit Mother became bolder and several times she asked to have whole symphonies and concertos played to us. We sat for nearly an hour cooped up in a tiny room with the salesman restlessly shuffling his feet, yawning and not knowing what to expect next. Mother pretended he hardly existed and, making herself comfortable in the cane chair, with a determined, intent expression she gazed straight ahead at the whirling disc.

We were soon known to everyone at the shops. Eyes lit up as we walked in, Mother looking neither this way nor that with two children walking in file through the passage-way towards the record department. I was very conscious of the humorous glances and the discreet sniggers that followed us and I would sometimes catch hold of Mother's hand and plead with her to leave the shop. But she paid no heed and we continued to our destination. The more often we came the more uncomfortably self-conscious I became and I dreaded the laughing faces round me.

Soon we became something more than a joke. The smiles turned to scowls and the shop attendants refused to play us any more records. The first time this happened the sales-man mumbled something and left us standing outside the door of the music-room.

Mother was not easily thwarted and without a trace of a smile she said we should talk to the manager. I was filled with a sense of shame and humiliation and with downcast eyes I sidled towards the entrance of the shop.

Mother caught up with me and, laying her hand upon my arm, she said, "What are you afraid of? Your mother won't disgrace you, believe me." Looking at me in her searching way she went on, "Think carefully. Who is right —are they or are we? Why shouldn't they play for us? Does it cost them anything? By which other way can we ever hope to hear something good? Just because we are poor must we cease our striving?"

She continued to talk in this way until I went back with her. The three of us walked into the manager's office and I translated Mother's words.

The manager was stern, though I imagine he must have had some difficulty in keeping his serious demeanour.

"But do you ever intend to buy any records?" he said after I had spoken.

"If I were a rich woman would you ask me that question?" Mother replied and I repeated her words in a halting voice.

"Speak up to him," she nudged me while I could feel my face fill with hot blood.

The manager repeated his first question and Mother, impatient at my hesitant tone, plunged into a long speech on our right to music and culture and in fact the rights of all men, speaking in her own tongue as though the manager understood every word. It was in vain; he merely shook his head.

We were barred from shop after shop, and in each case Mother made a stand, arguing at length until the man in charge flatly told us not to come back until we could afford to buy records.

We met with rebuffs in other places as well.

Once as we wandered through the university, my sister

and I sauntering behind while Mother opened doors, listening to lectures for brief moments, we unexpectedly found ourselves in a large room where white-coated young men and women sat on high stools in front of arrays of tubes, beakers and jars.

Mother's eyes lit up brightly and she murmured something about knowledge and science. We stood close to her and gazed round in astonishment; neither her words nor what we saw conveyed anything to us. She wanted to go round the room but a gentleman wearing a black gown came up and asked us if we were looking for someone. He was a distinguished looking person with a florid face and a fine grey mane.

Repeating Mother's words I said, "We are not looking for anyone; we are simply admiring this room of knowledge."

The gentleman's face wrinkled pleasantly. With a tiny smile playing over his lips he said regretfully that we could not stay, since only students were permitted in the room.

As I interpreted his words Mother's expression changed. Her sallow face was almost red. For ten full seconds she looked the gentleman in the eyes. Then she said rapidly to me, "Ask him why he speaks with such a condescending smile on his face."

I said, "My mother asks why you talk with such a superior smile on your face?"

He coughed, shifted his feet restlessly and his face set severely. Then he glared at his watch and without another word walked away with dignified steps.

When we came out into the street a spring day was in its full beauty. Mother sighed to herself and after a moment's silence said, "That fine professor thinks he is a liberal-minded man, but behind his smile he despises people such as us. You will have to struggle here just as hard as I had to back home. For all the fine talk it is like all other countries. But where are the people with ideals like those back home, who aspire to something better?"

She repeated those words frequently, even when I was a boy of thirteen and I knew so much more about the new country that was my home. Then I could argue with her.

I said to her that Benny who lived in our street was always reading books and papers and hurrying to meetings. Benny was not much older than I was and he had many friends whom he met in the park on Sunday. They all belonged to this country and they were interested in all the things Mother talked about.

"Benny is an exception," she said with an impatient shrug of her shoulders, "and his friends are only a tiny handful." Then she added, "And what about you? You and your companions only worship bats and balls as heathens do stone idols. Why, in the old country boys of your age took part in the fight to deliver mankind from oppression! They gave everything, their strength and health, even their lives, for that glorious ideal."

"That's what Benny wants to do," I said, pleased to be able to answer Mother.

"But it's so different here. Even your Benny will be swallowed up in the smug, smooth atmosphere. You wait and see."

She spoke obstinately. It seemed impossible to change her. Her vision was too much obscured by passionate dreams of the past for her to see any hope in the present, in the new land.

But as an afterthought she added, "Perhaps it is different for those like you and Benny. But for me I can never find my way into this life here."

She turned away, her narrow back stooped, her gleaming black hair curled into a bun on her short, thin neck, her shoes equally down at heel on each side.

## OTHER TITLES IN THE
## IMPRINT CLASSICS SERIES

### INTIMATE STRANGERS

*Katharine Susannah Prichard*

Greg and Elodie have reached that point in a marriage when passion gives way to habit and the pleasures of a shared life become monotonous.

For Greg diversion is possible in discreet liaisons, but when temptation comes to Elodie, it threatens to overwhelm them both.

Set against the political turmoil of the Depression, *Intimate Strangers* is a frank account of marital breakdown, and explores the choices a woman can make, and should make: as wife, mother and lover.

*Intimate Strangers* is published here with an introduction by Ric Throssell.

## THE TIMELESS LAND

### *Eleanor Dark*

First published in 1941, Eleanor Dark's classic novel of the early settlement of Australia is a story of hardship, cruelty and danger. Above all it is the story of conflict: between the Aborigines and the white settlers.

In this dramatic novel, introduced here by Humphrey McQueen, a large cast of characters, historical and fictional, black and white, convict and settler, brings alive those bitter years with moments of tenderness and conciliation amid the brutality and hostility. All the while, behind the veneer of British civilisation, lies the baffling presence of Australia, a timeless land that shares with England 'not even its seasons or its stars'.

## MY BRILLIANT CAREER
### MY CAREER GOES BUNG

*Miles Franklin*

'I am given to something which a man never pardons in a woman. You will draw away as though I were a snake when you hear.'

With this warning, Sybylla confesses to her rich and handsome suitor that she is *given to writing stories,* and bound, therefore, on a brilliant career.

In this ironically titled and exuberant first novel by Miles Franklin, originally published in 1901, Sybylla tells the story of growing up passionate and rebellious in rural New South Wales, where the most girls could hope for was to marry or to teach. Sybylla will do neither, but that doesn't stop her from falling in love, and it doesn't make the choices any easier.

For the first time ever, *My Brilliant Career* is published with its sequel, *My Career Goes Bung.* It is introduced by Elizabeth Webby.

# WATERWAY

## *Eleanor Dark*

This sparkling novel, set on the edge of Sydney harbour, follows a small group of people through the intricacies of a single day; a day that reaches its climax on the harbour when the ferry bound for Watson's Bay collides with a liner and sinks.

How will the accident change the life of Winifred, married to vindictive Arthur and in love with Ian? Will the events of the day alter the resentments of Jack Saunders or the vanities of Lorna Sellman? Is there any reason or morality when it comes to accident and death?

First published in 1938 when Eleanor Dark was at the heart of her powers, and reprinted here with an introduction by Drusilla Modjeska, *Waterway* is as brightly patterned as the harbour and as full of life as the people it describes.